HOW TO DRAW ANIMALS

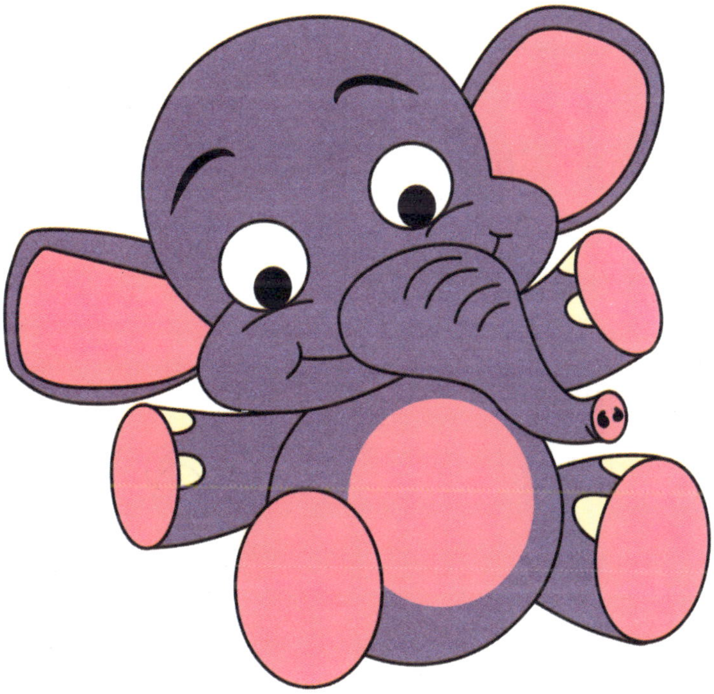

Om KIDZ

An imprint of Om Books International

Dog

STEP 1 2 3 4

A dog is called a man's best friend. It makes a good pet because it is intelligent, loyal and trustworthy.

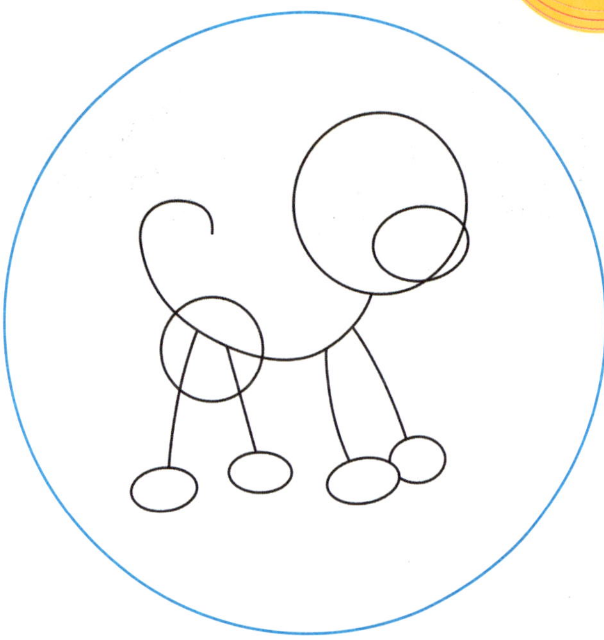

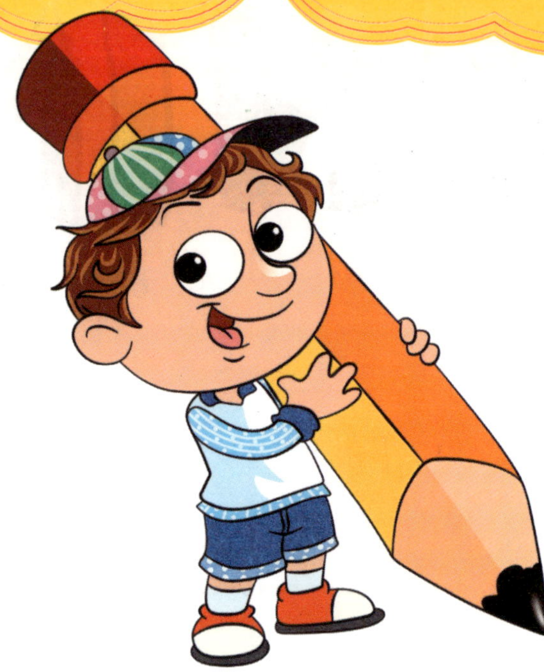

1. Draw a small circle with a big circle around it for the face. Draw in circles for its paws. Draw lines for the legs and another circle for the lower body and tail.

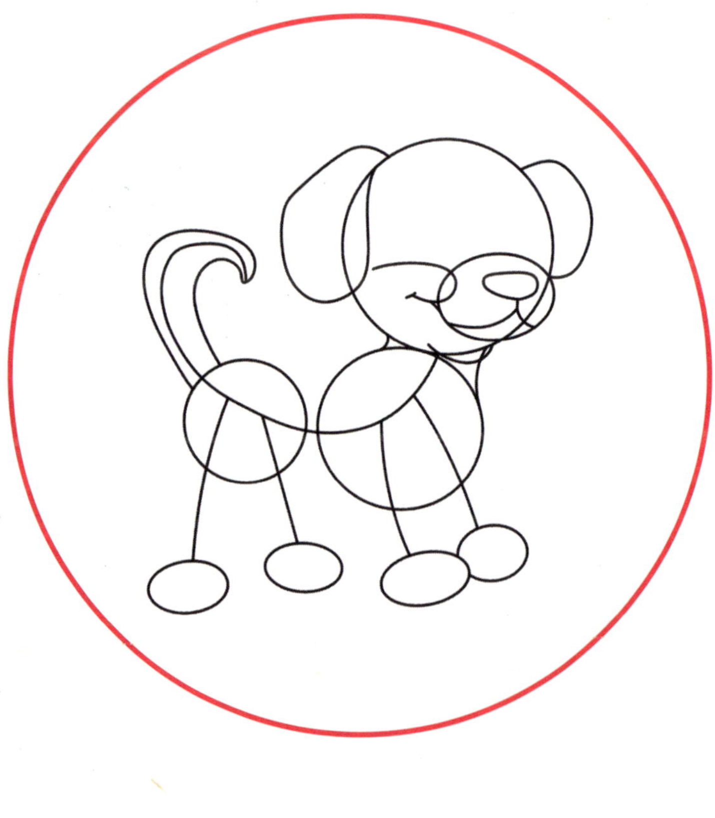

2. Draw the tail and the ears. Draw a circle for upper body. Draw its nose and mouth.

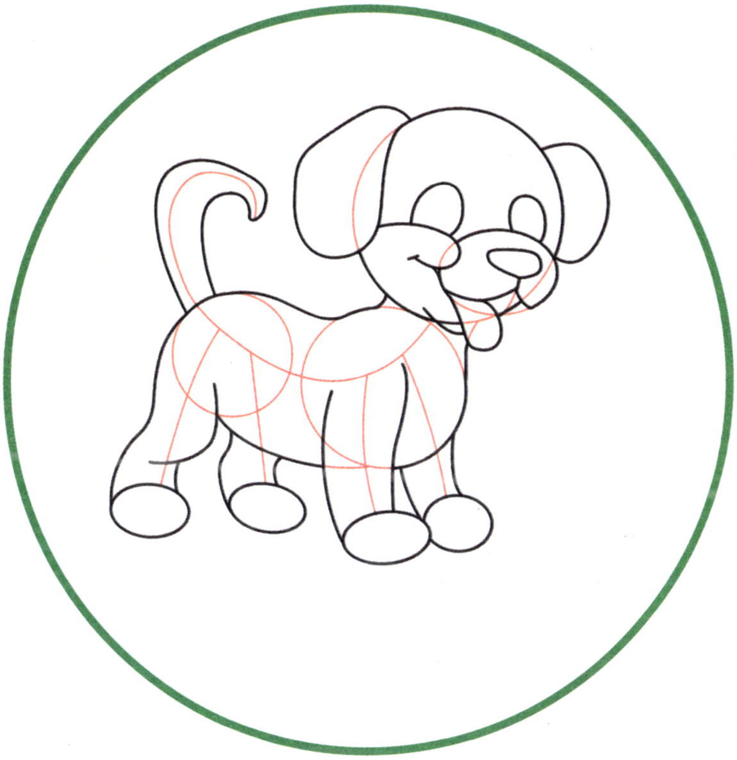

3 Draw its eyes, nose and tongue and face. Draw the legs, paws and body. Erase the unwanted lines (marked in red).

4 Fill in eyes. Draw lines for the paws and eyebrows.

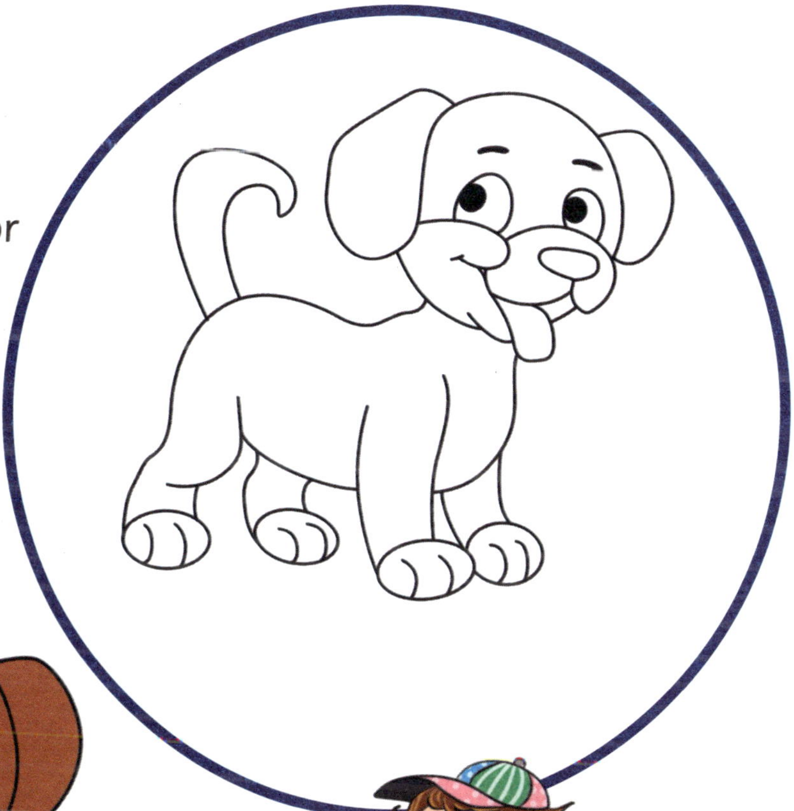

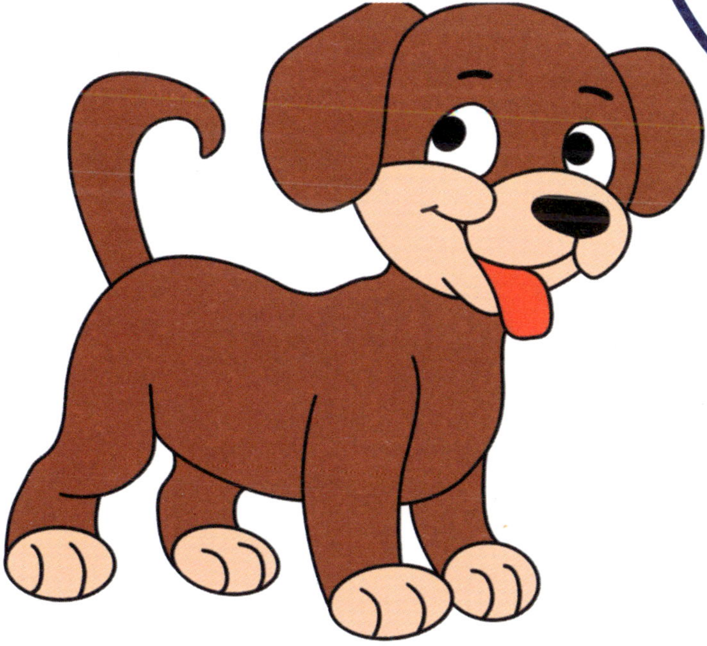

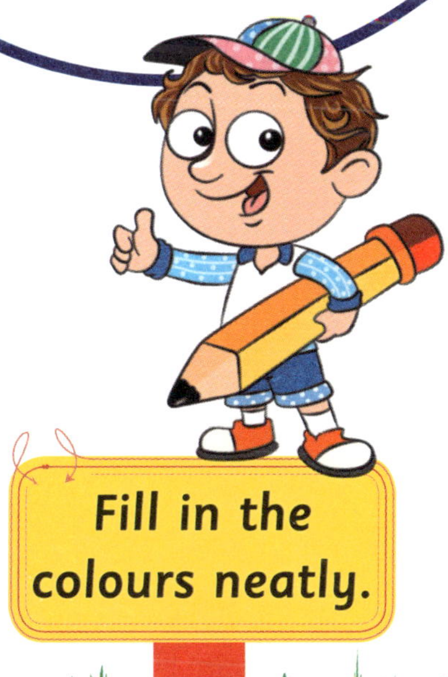

Cat

STEP 1 2 3 4

A cat is a small animal. It loves to drink milk.

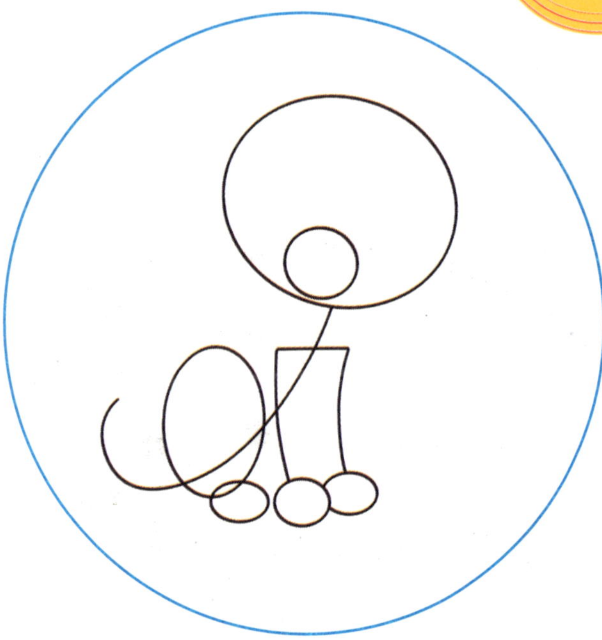

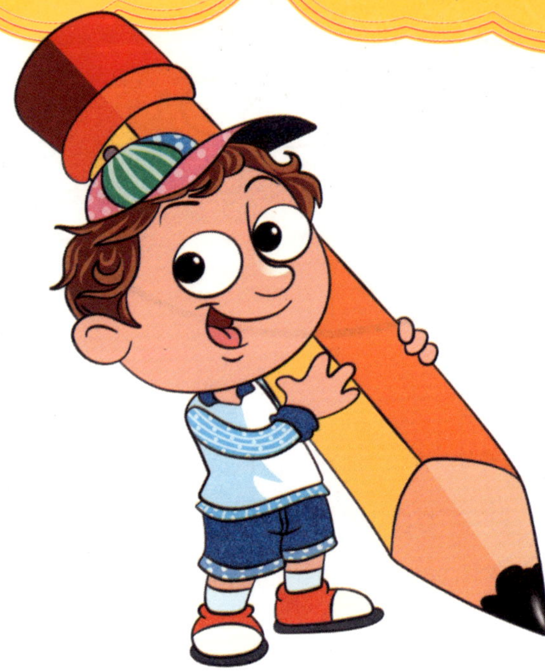

1 Draw a small circle and a big circle around it. Then a small rectangle and an oval below with small circles under it. Draw lines for the body and tail.

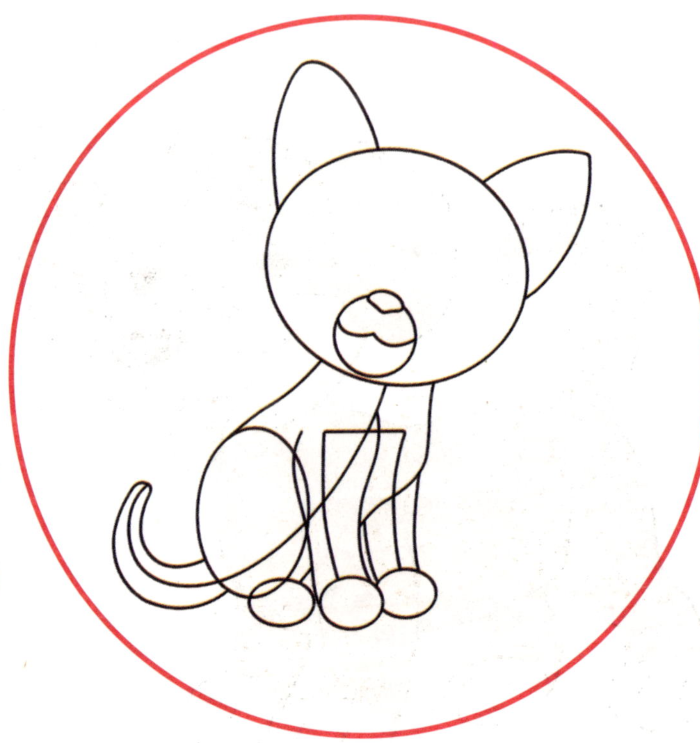

2 Draw in the ears, face and tail. Draw in the mouth, nose, legs and body.

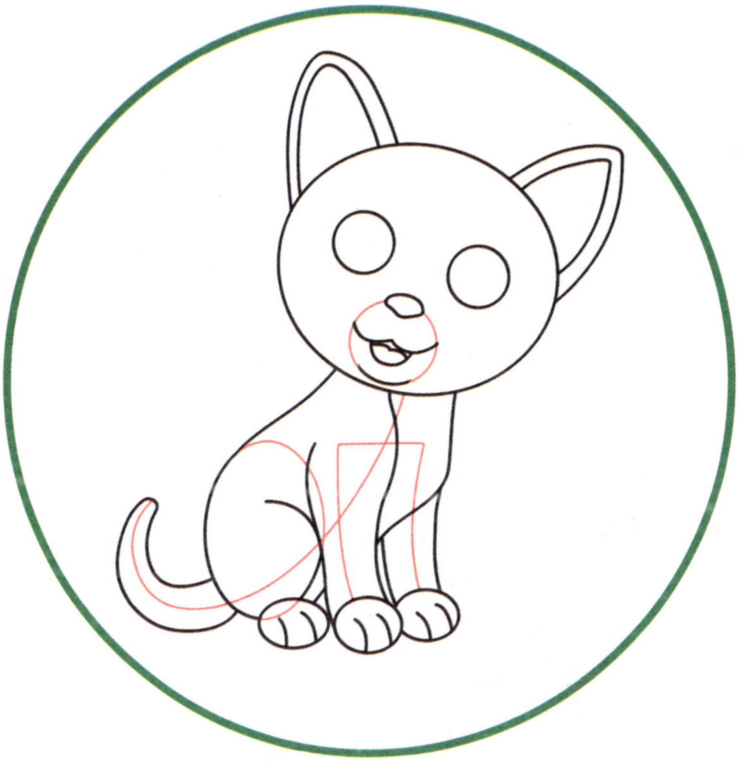

3. Draw the inside of the ears and its eyes and mouth. Draw its paws. Erase the unwanted lines (marked in red).

4. Draw its eyes, tooth and eyebrows. Draw in the stripes and the whiskers.

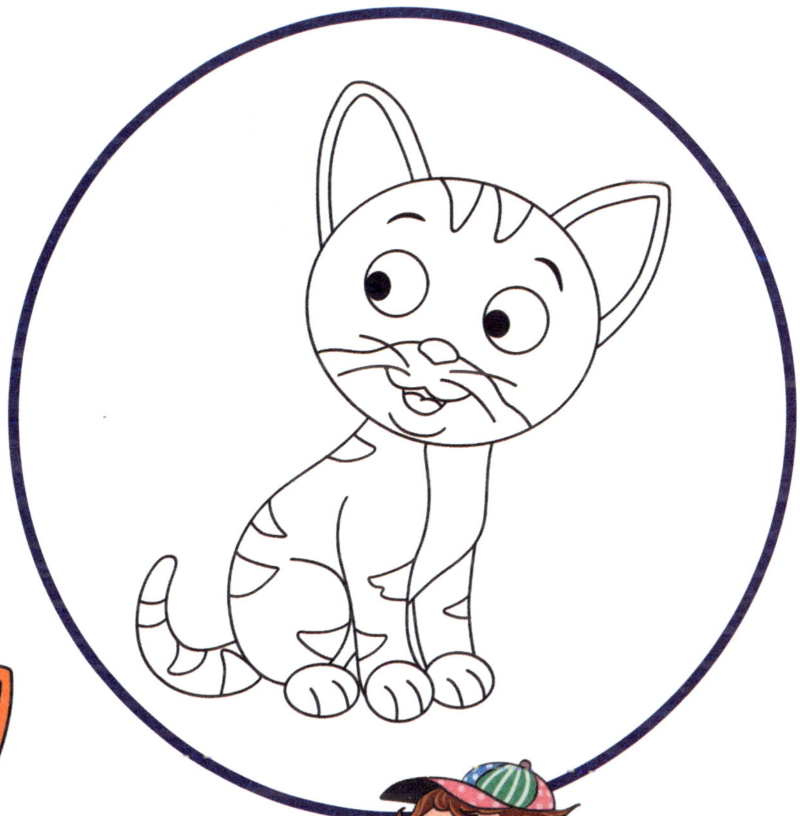

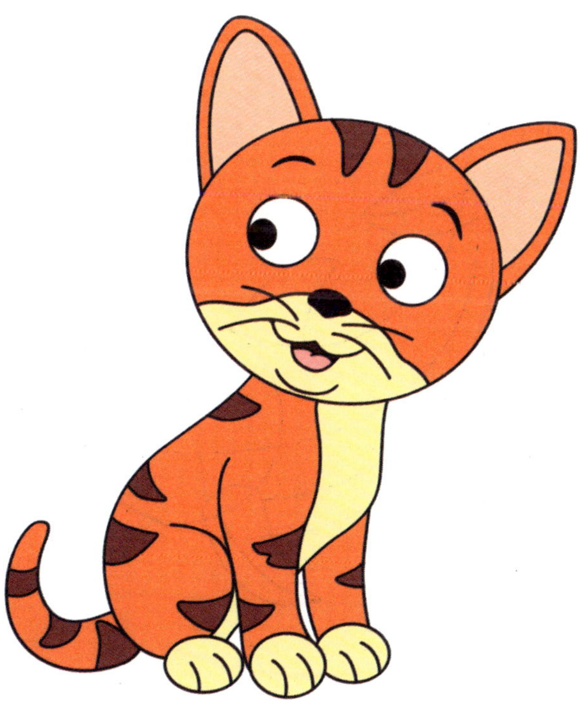

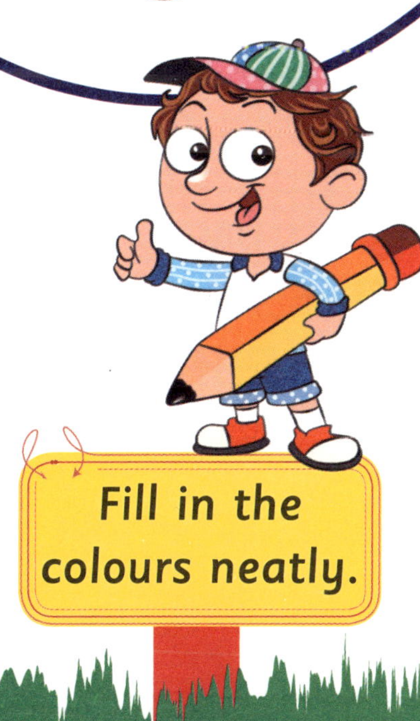

Dolphin

STEP 1 2 3 4

A dolphin is a mammal, just like a human being. It is one of the most intelligent marine creatures.

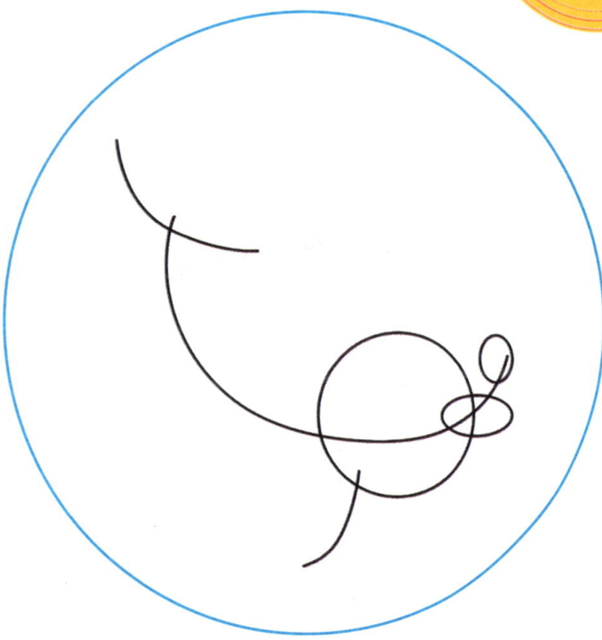

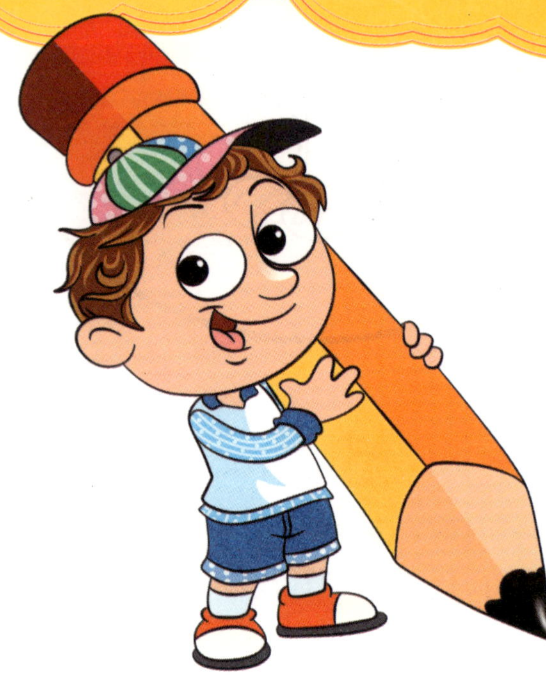

1. Draw circles for the face. Draw a circle and an oval for the mouth. Draw lines for the body, tail and fin.

2. Draw its tail, body, fins and mouth.

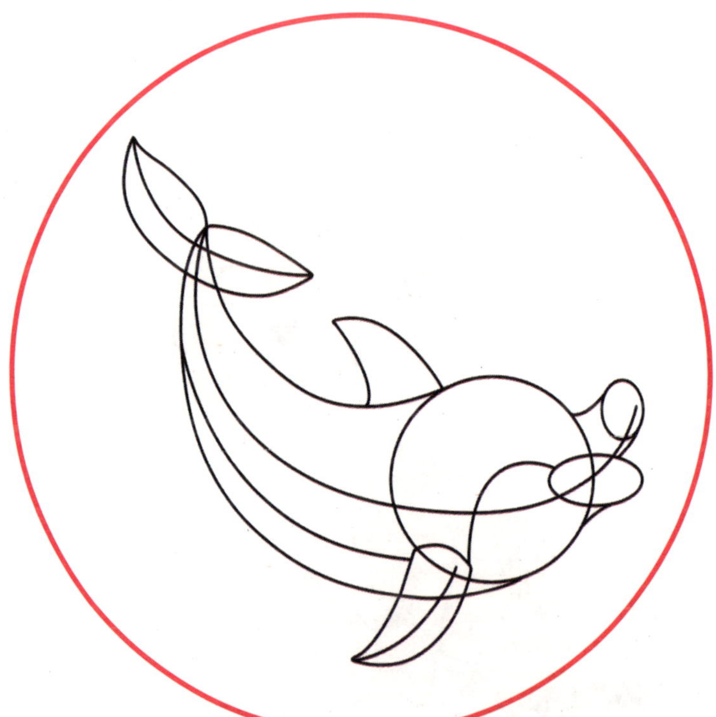

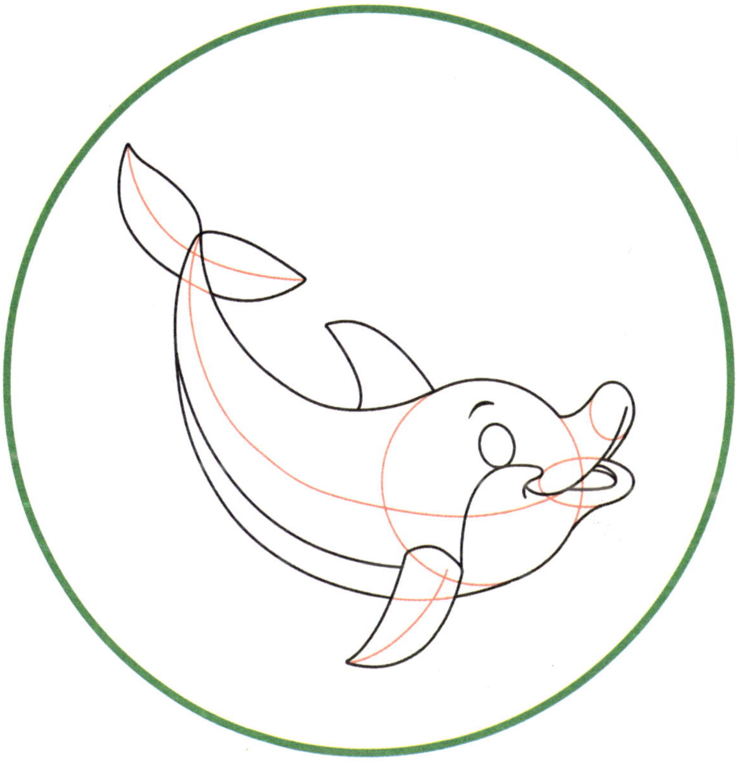

3 Draw in its face, eye, eyebrow, tongue and mouth.
Erase the unwanted lines (marked in red).

4 Fill in details of its eye.

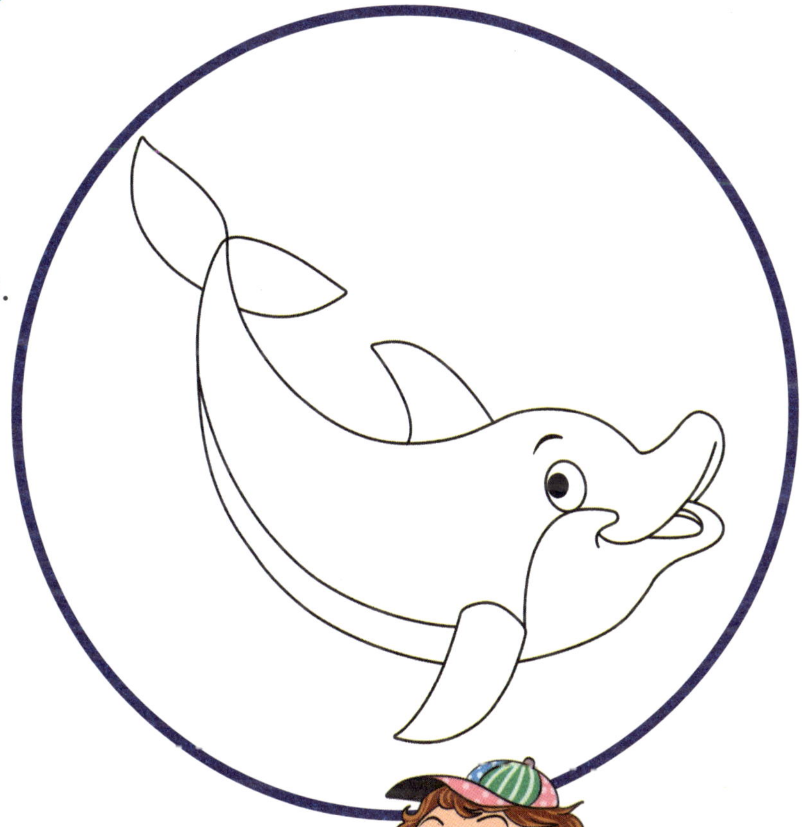

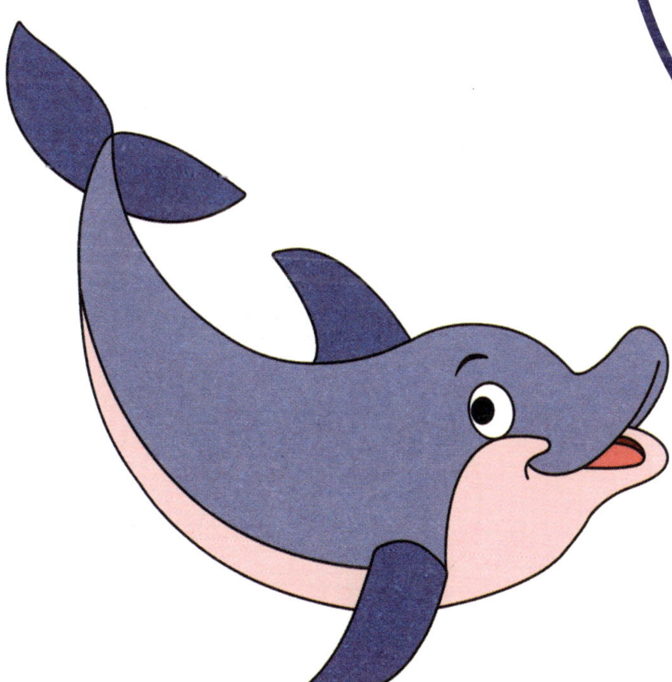

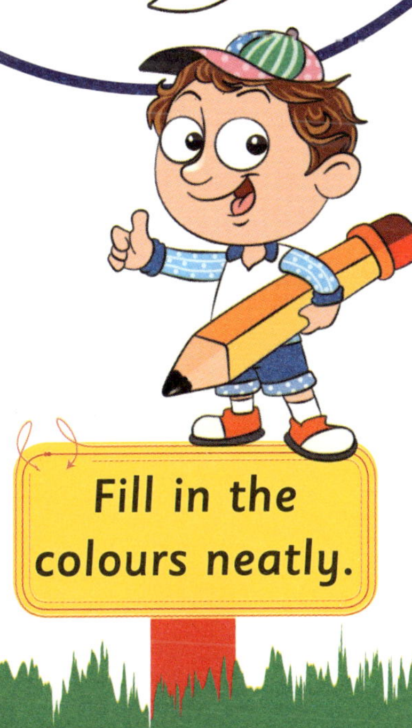

Elephant

STEP 1 2 3 4

An elephant has a really good memory and is very intelligent. It has a long trunk and a short tail.

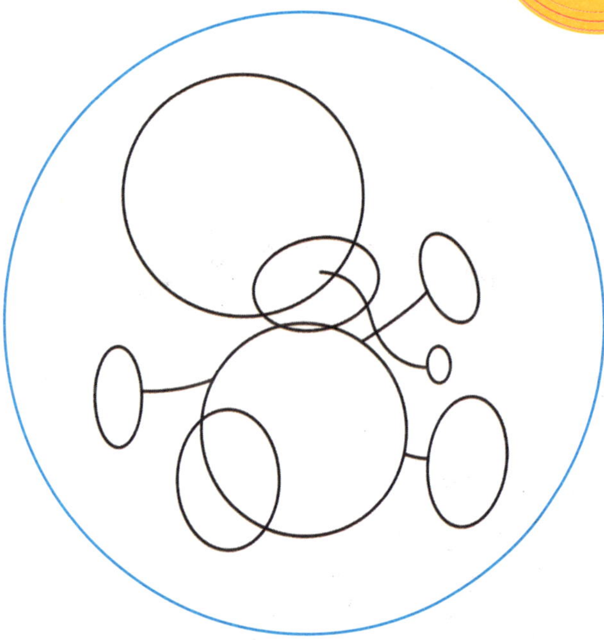

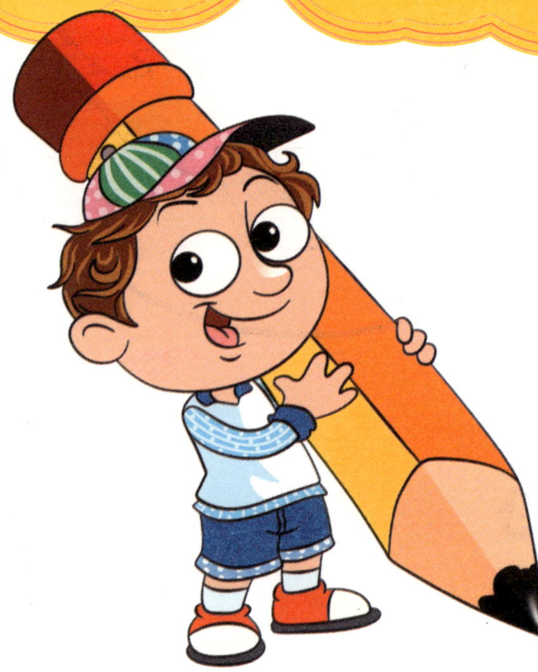

1. Draw a circle with an oval inside it and a line with a circle at its end for the face and trunk. Draw another circle for the body and more circles with lines for the arms and legs.

2. Use circles and lines to draw its face, trunk and ears.

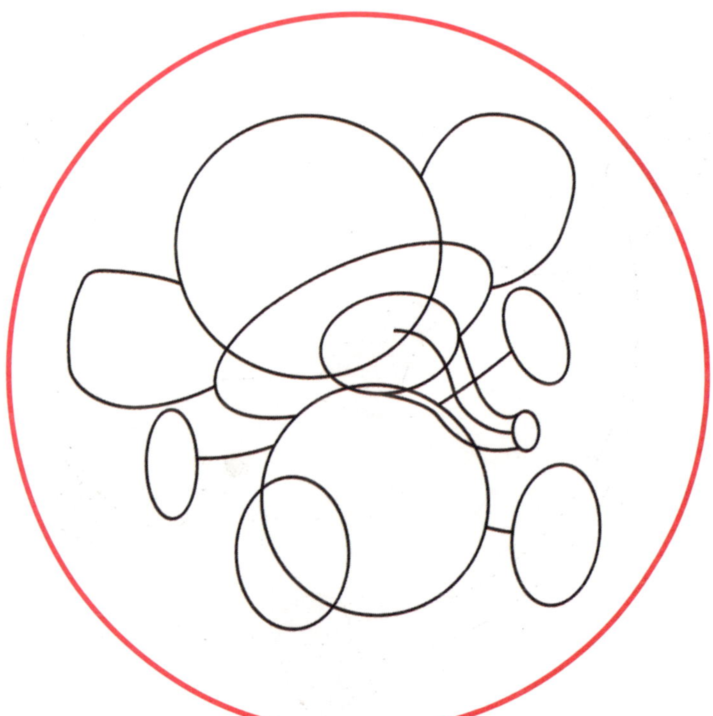

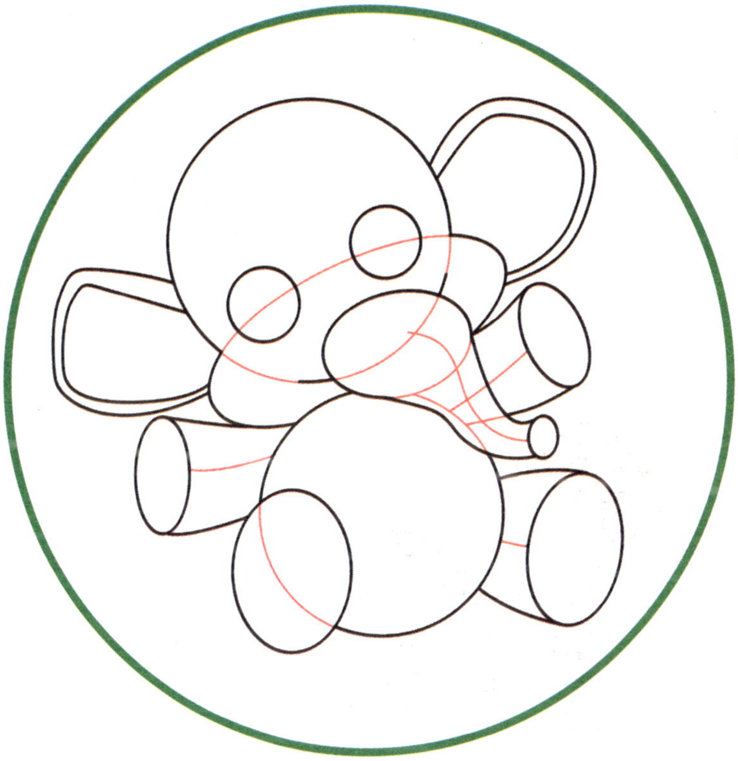

3 Draw in the eyes and the inside of the ears. Draw in the arms and legs.
Erase the unwanted lines (marked in red).

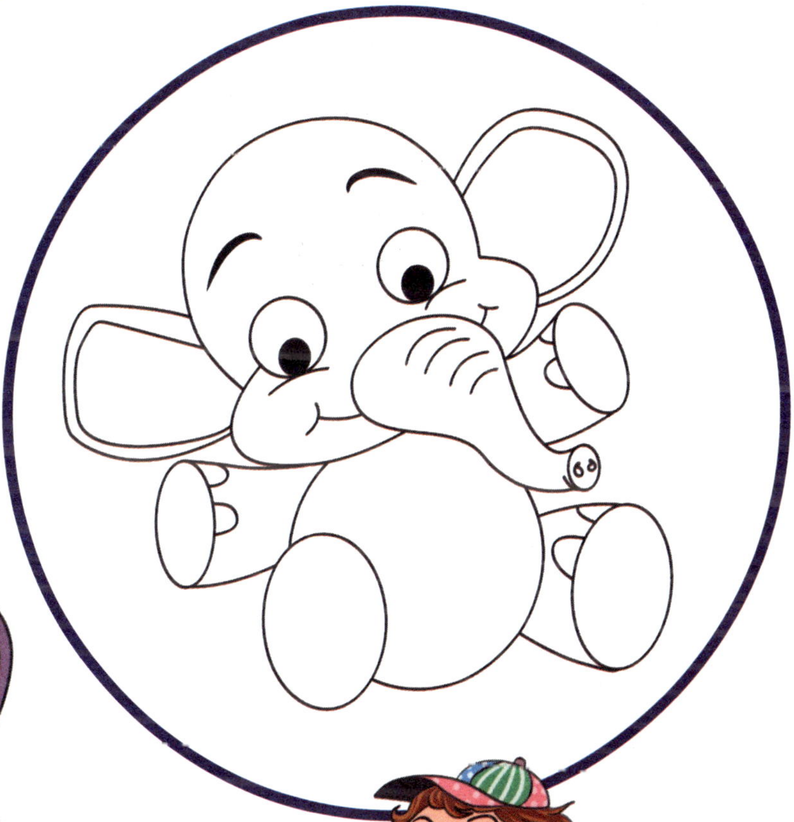

4 Fill in its eyes. Draw in its eyebrows and mouth. Put in the details of its trunk, arms and legs.

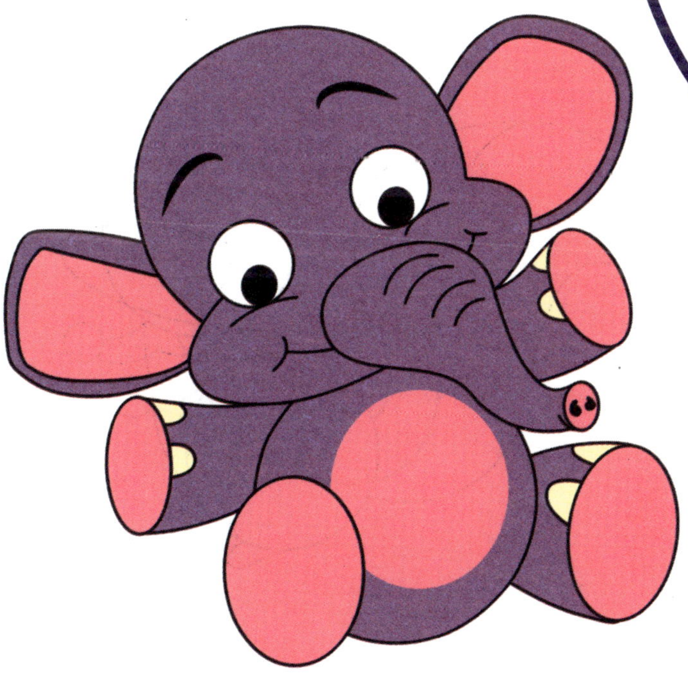

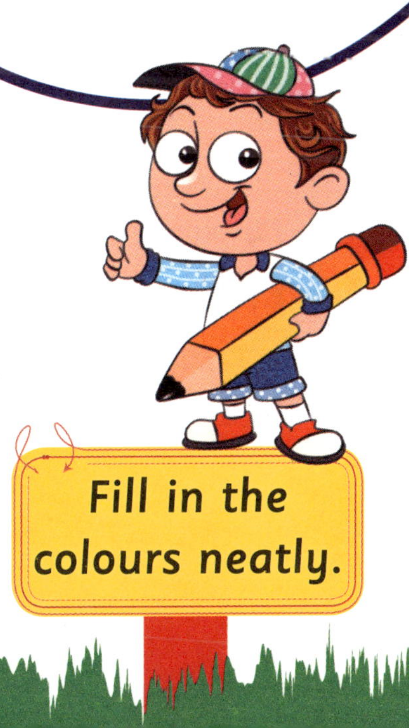

Squirrel

STEP 1 2 3 4

A squirrel has big eyes and a long bushy tail. It loves eating nuts.

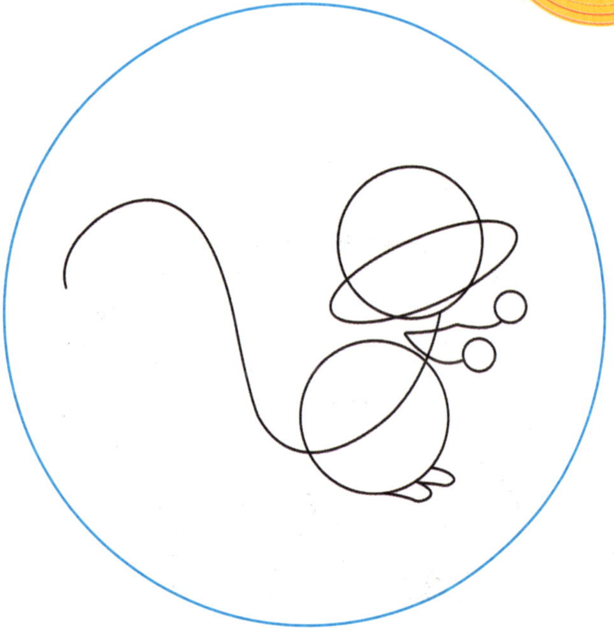

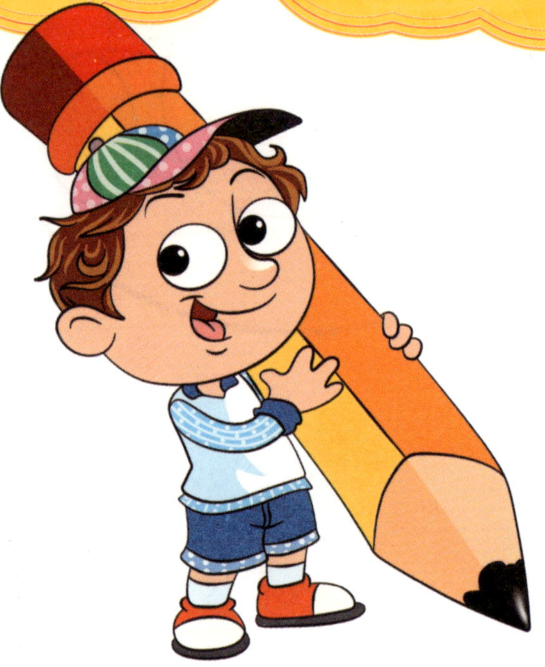

1 Draw circles for the face and lower body. Draw lines for the upper body and the tail. Draw ovals for its feet and circles joined with lines for its arms.

2 Draw in its nose, arms, body and tail.

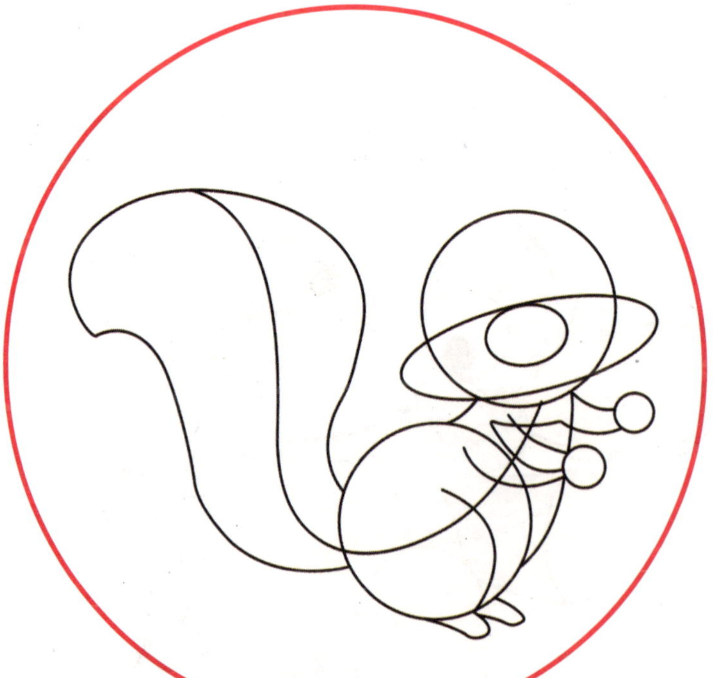

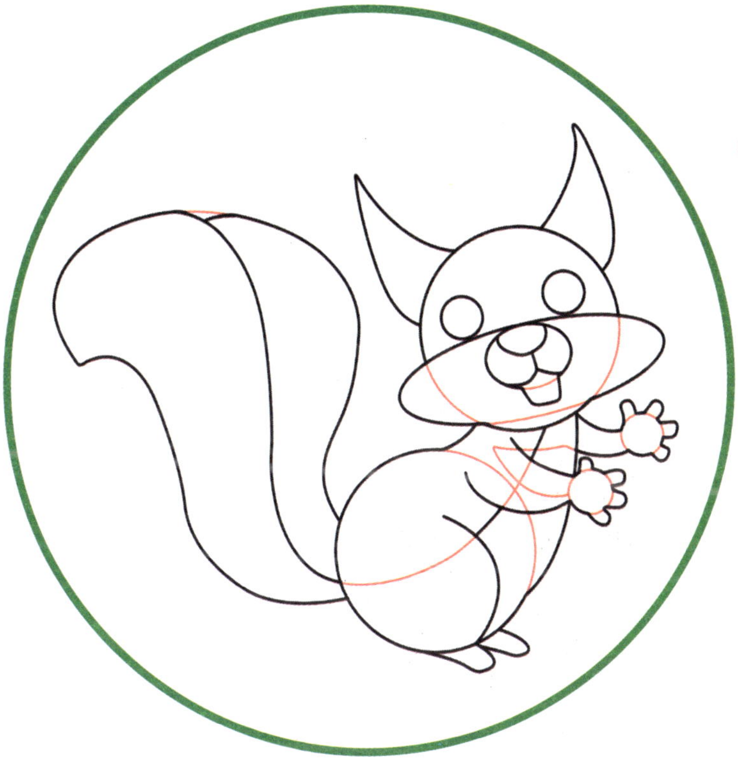

3 Draw in the eyes, hands, mouth, ears and nose. Erase the unwanted lines (marked in red).

4 Draw in the insides of its eyes and ears. Draw in its eyebrows, teeth and feet.

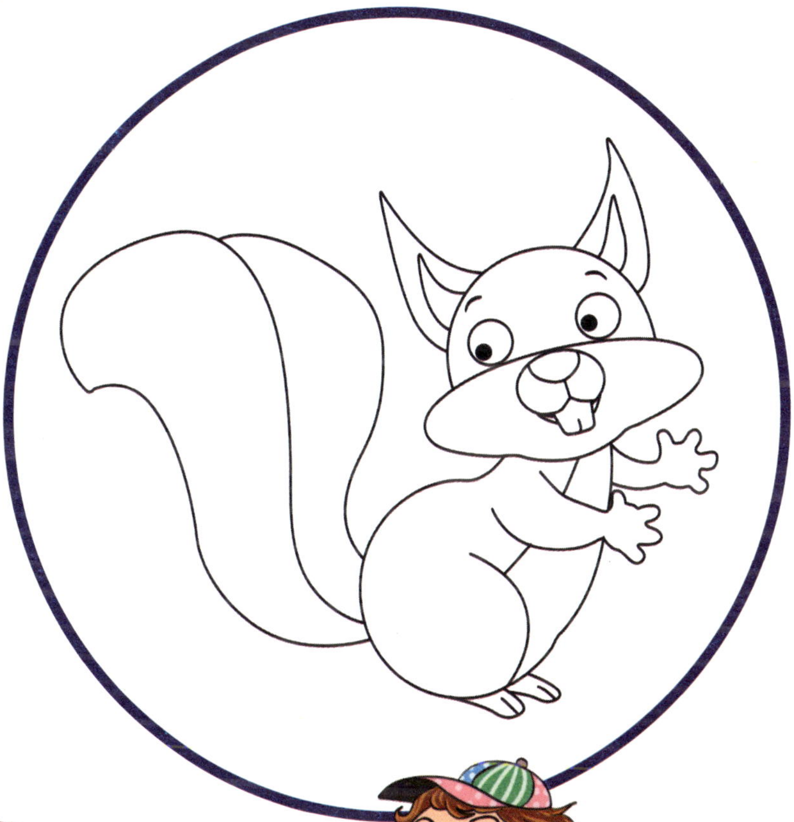

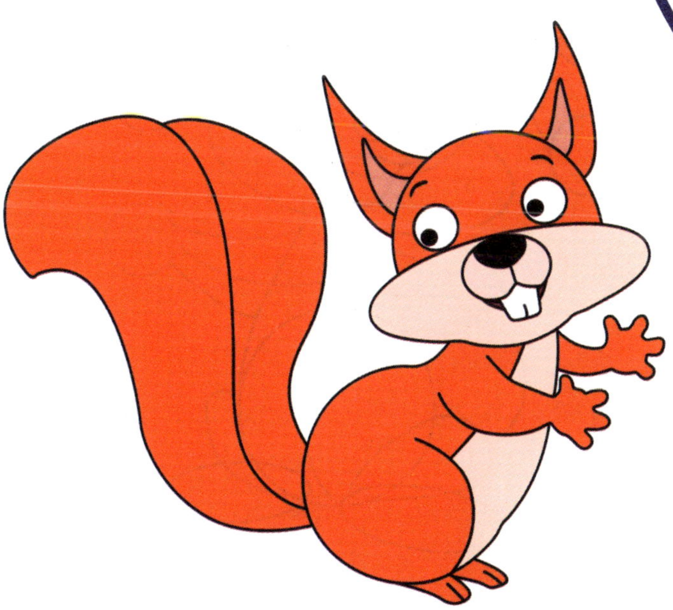

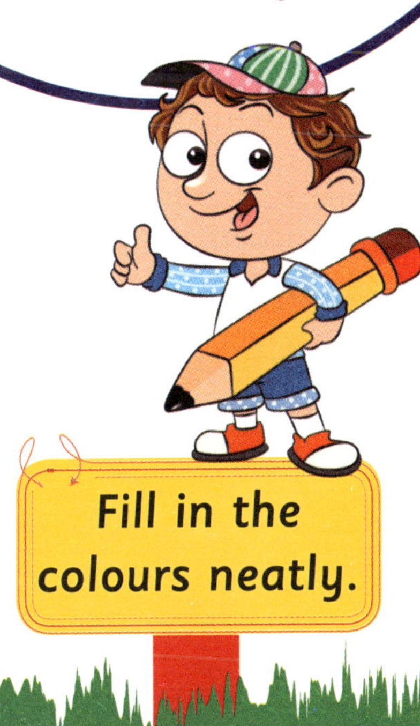

Rabbit

STEP 1 2 3 4

A rabbit is cute and fluffy. It loves eating carrots.

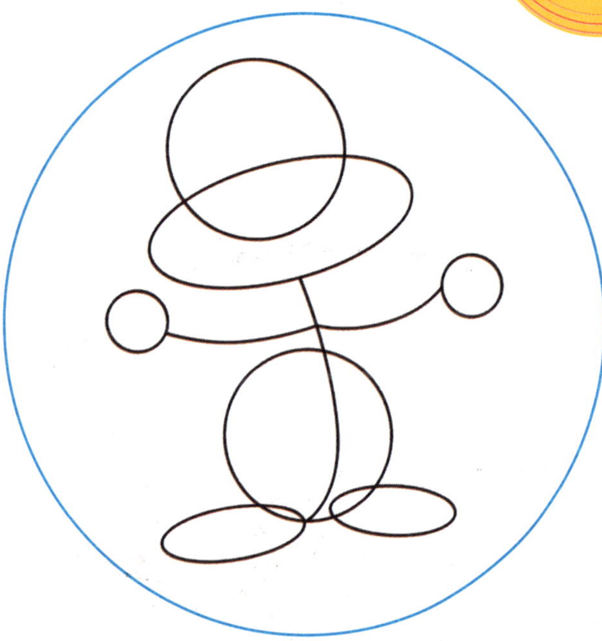

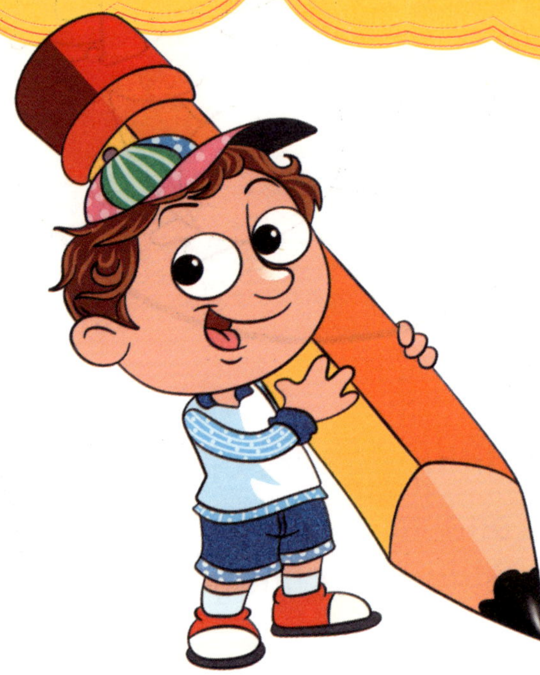

1. Draw circles for the face, lower body, hands and feet. Draw in lines for the arms, neck and upper body.

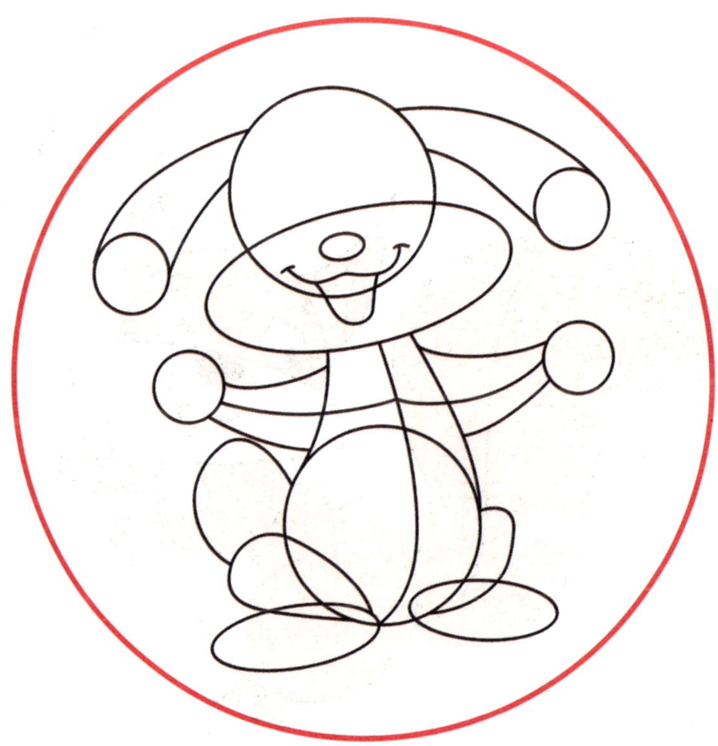

2. Draw its ears, nose, mouth, arms, body, tail, legs and feet.

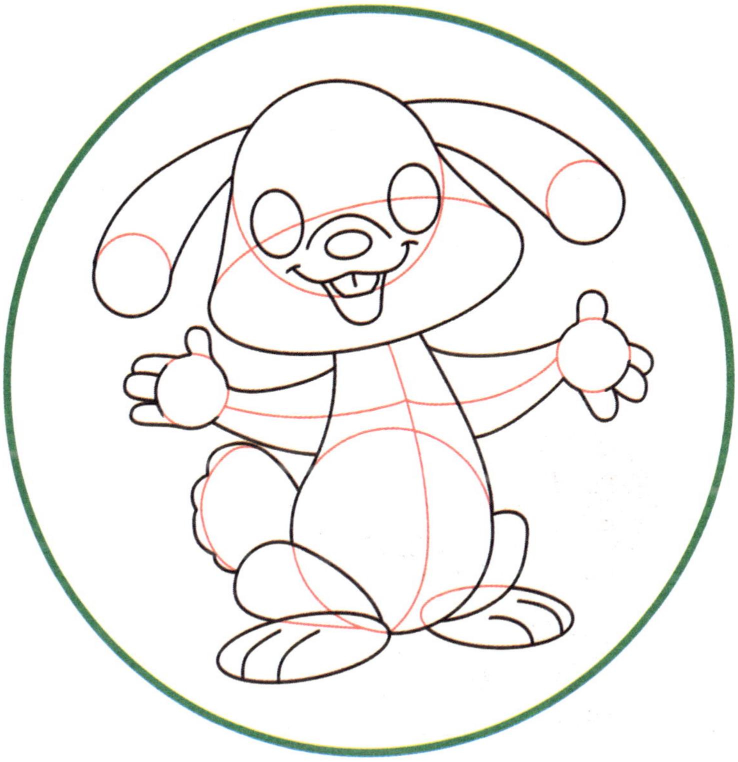

3 Draw in its eyes, teeth, hands, tail, legs and feet.
Erase the unwanted lines (marked in red).

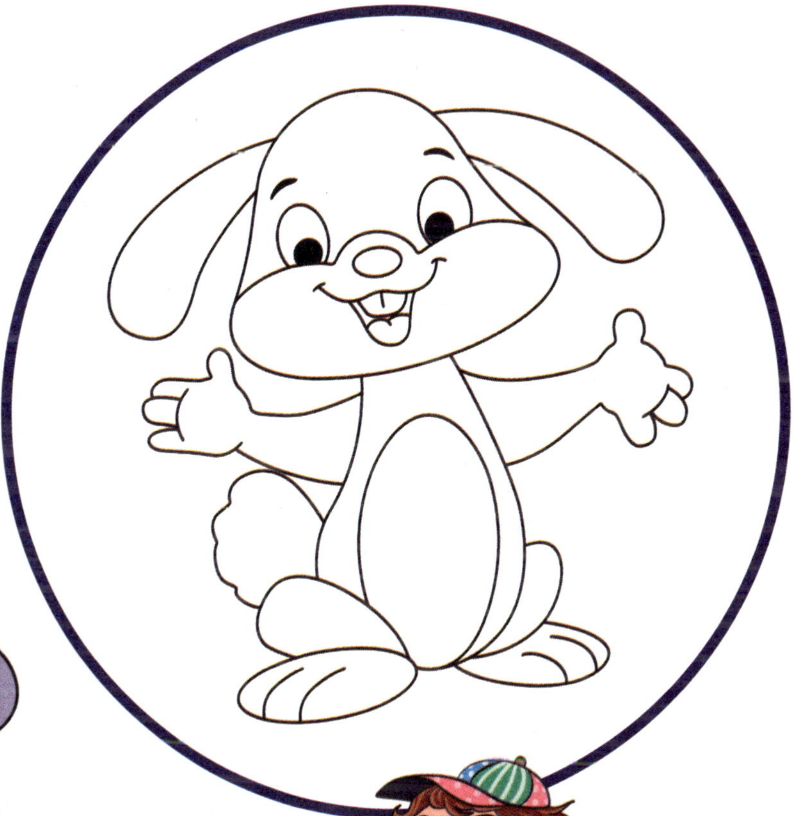

4 Fill in the eyes, eyebrows and lines of its face. Draw in the tongue and lines of its body.

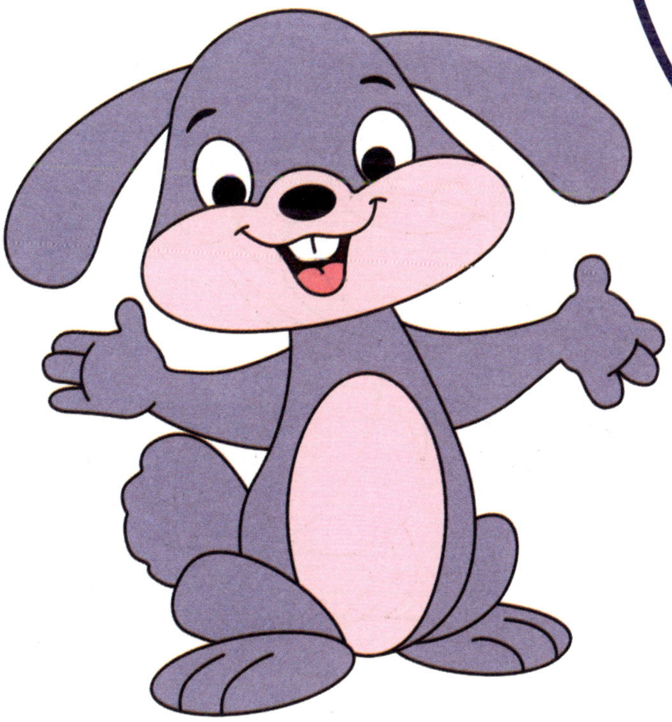

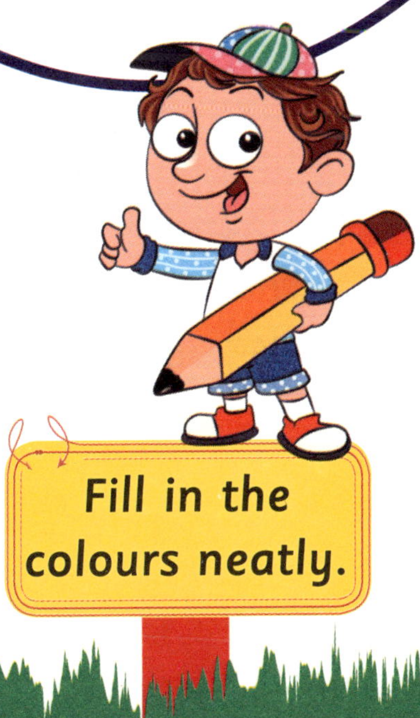

Monkey

STEP 1 2 3 4

A monkey is known for imitating us. It loves eating bananas.

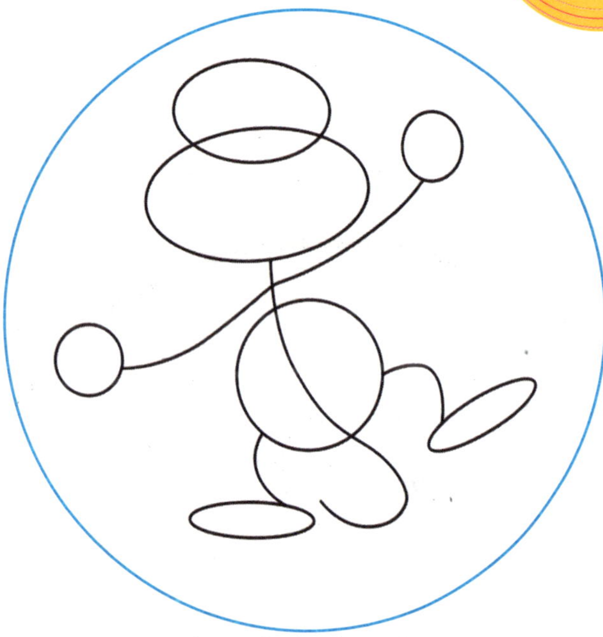

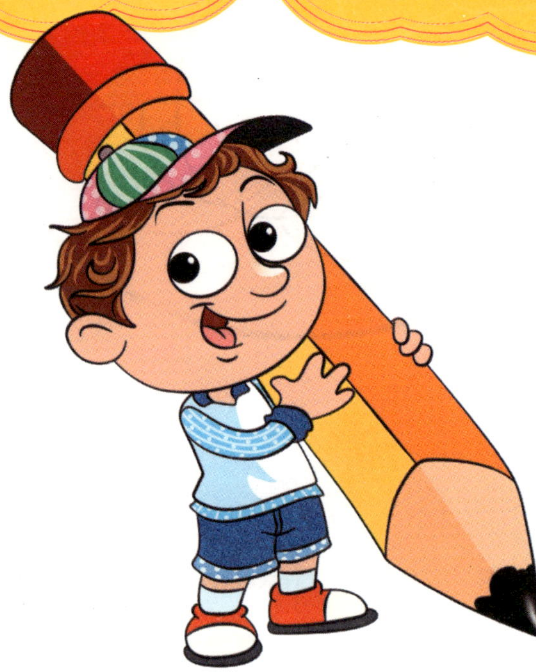

1. Draw circles for the face. Draw circles and lines for the arms, legs, body, feet and tail.

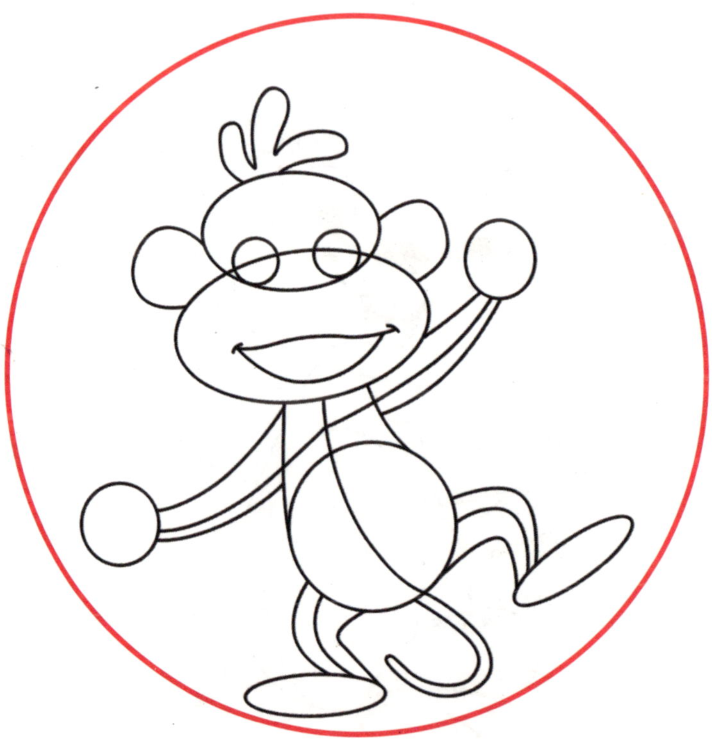

2. Draw its ears, eyes, hair, arms, body, legs, feet and tail.

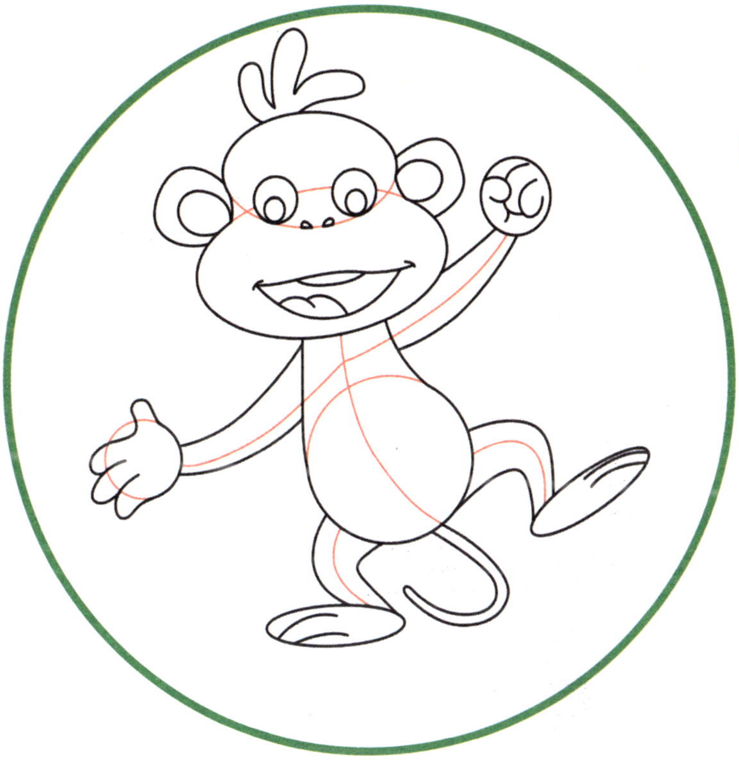

3 Draw the inside of its eyes, ears and dots for its nose. Draw its teeth and tongue. Draw in its hands and lines of its feet. Erase the unwanted lines (marked in red).

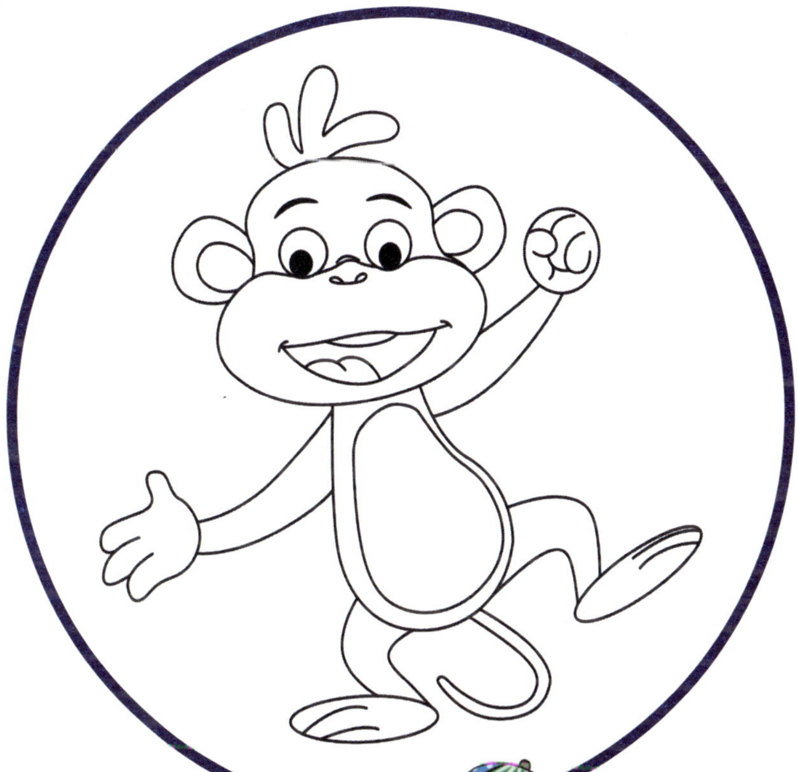

4 Add in the eyebrows and lines for the face and body.

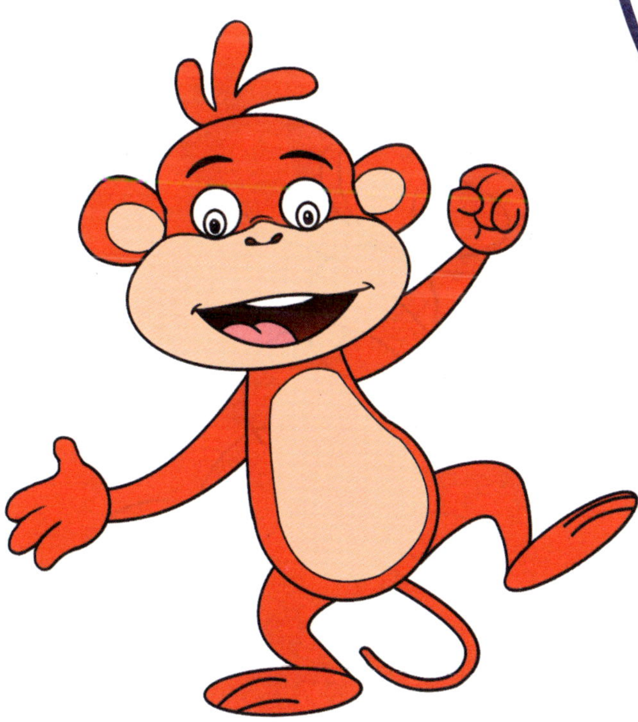

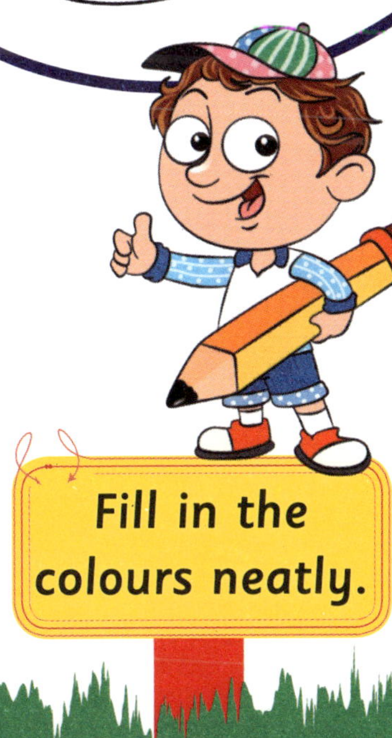

Mouse

STEP 1 2 3 4

A mouse loves cheese. It is also a popular character in many stories.

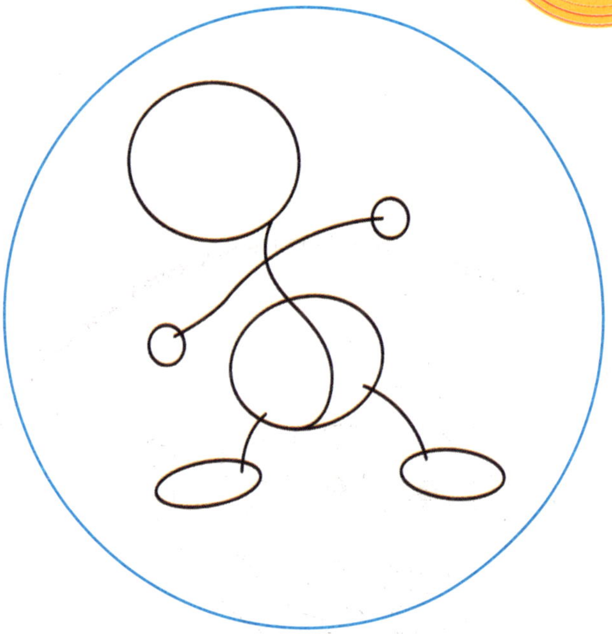

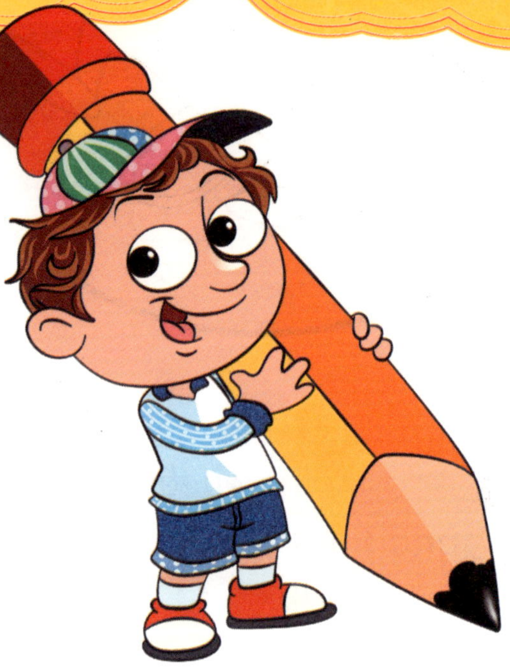

1. Draw circles for the head, lower body, hands and feet. Draw lines for the arms, neck, upper body and legs.

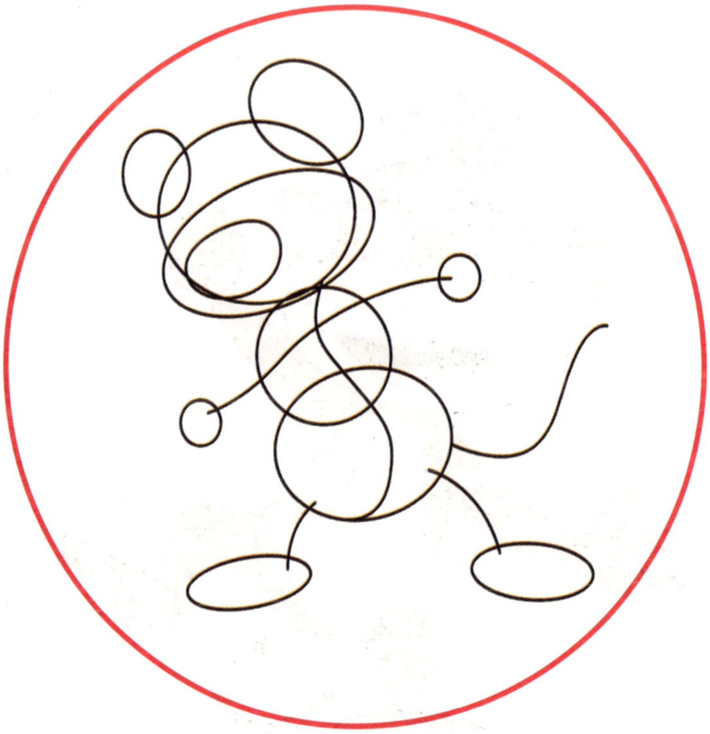

2. Add more circles for the face, ears and upper body and a line for a tail.

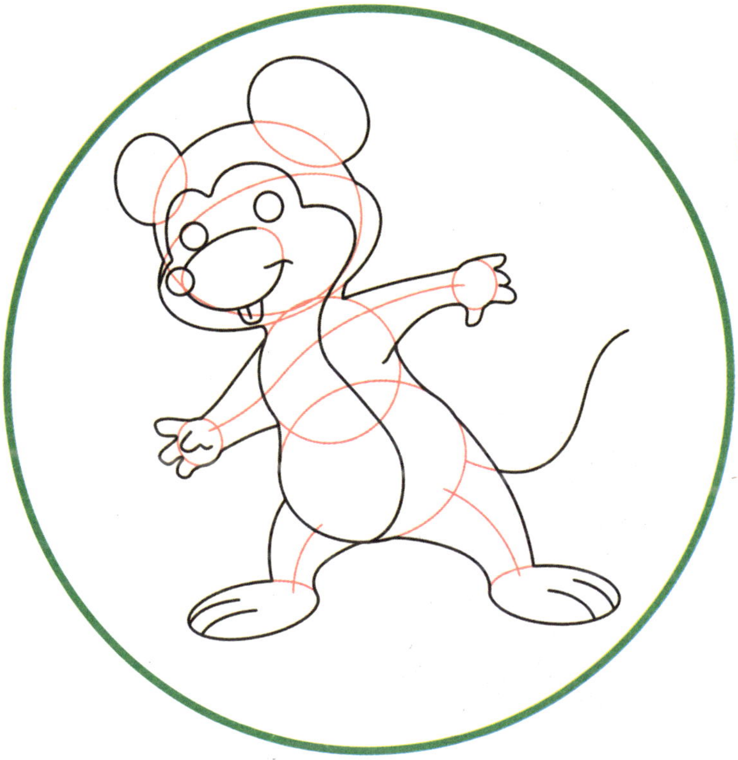

3 Draw in the face, eyes, mouth, nose and teeth. Draw the arms, legs, hands, feet, body and ears. Erase the unwanted lines (marked in red).

4 Fill in the eyes and insides of the ears. Draw in the eyebrows and the tail.

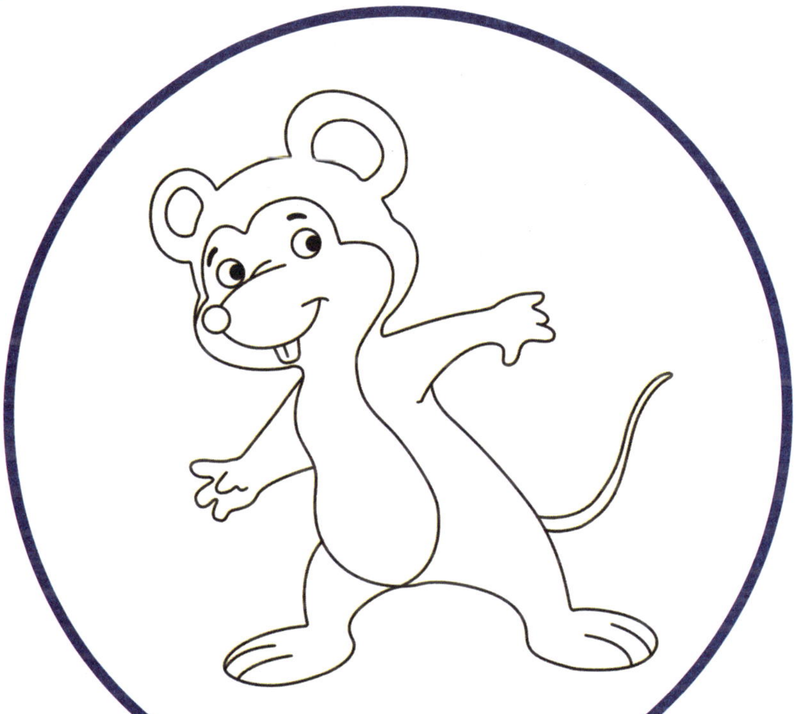

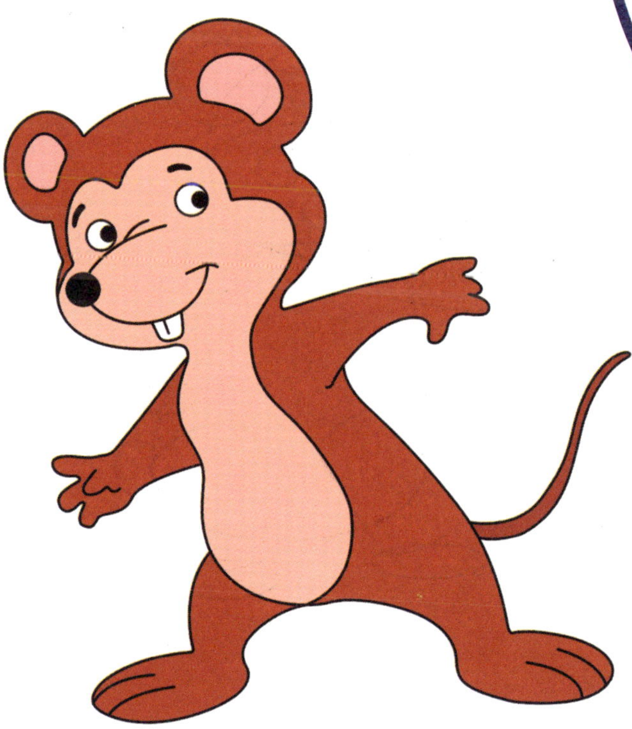

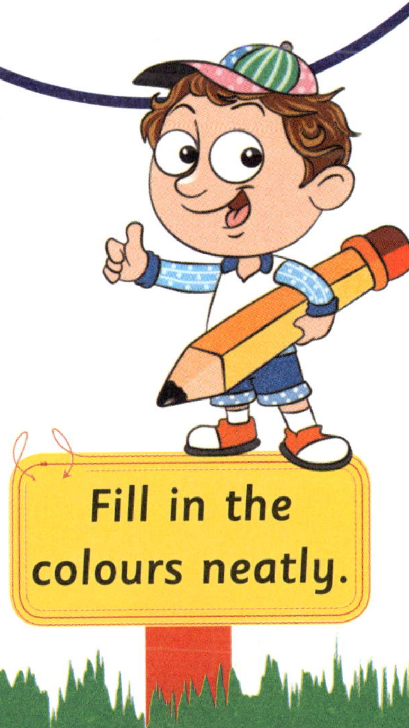

Bear

STEP 1 2 3 4

It is a big and strong animal. It sleeps for almost six months in winters.

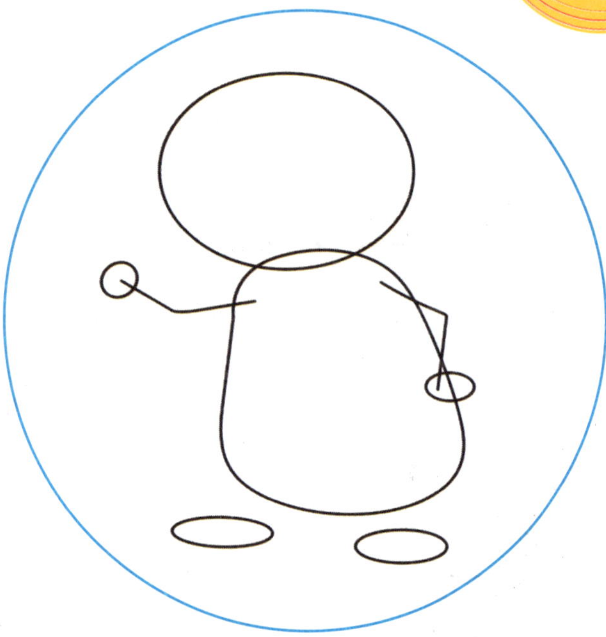

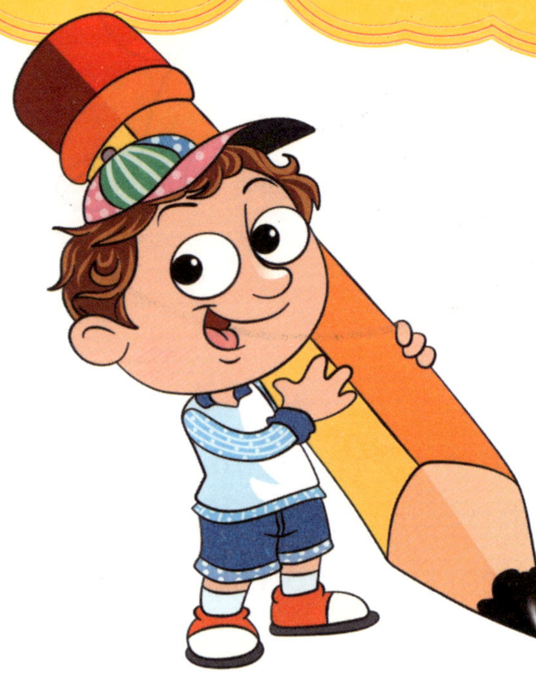

1. Draw a circle for the face and a curved egg-shape for the body. Draw two ovals for the feet and two small circles for the paws joined by lines to the body.

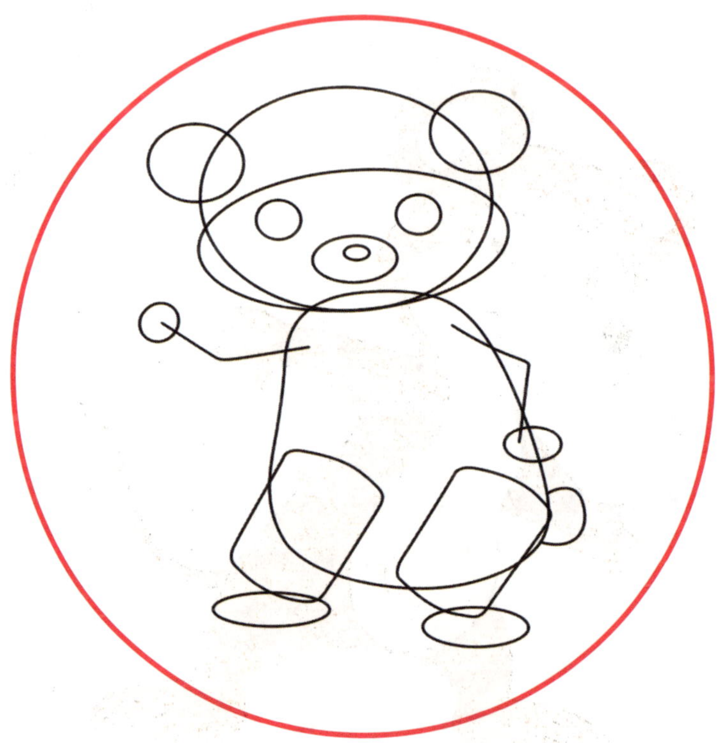

2. Draw its eyes and nose. Draw small circles for the face, ears and tail and curved rectangles for the legs.

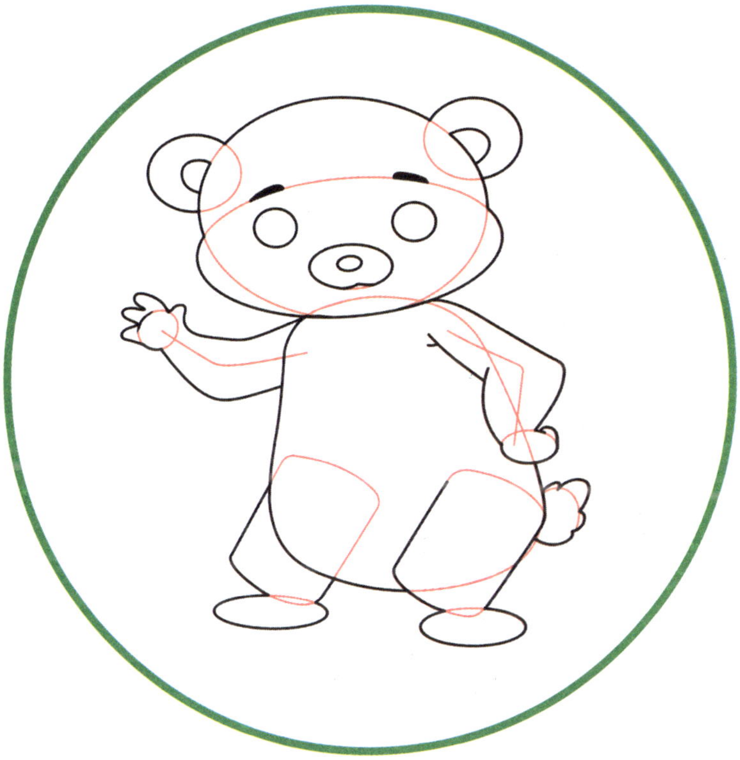

3 Draw the eyebrows, arms, paws, legs, and tail. Draw the inside of the ears.
Erase the unwanted lines (marked in red).

4 Fill in the eyes and add lines to its body and feet.

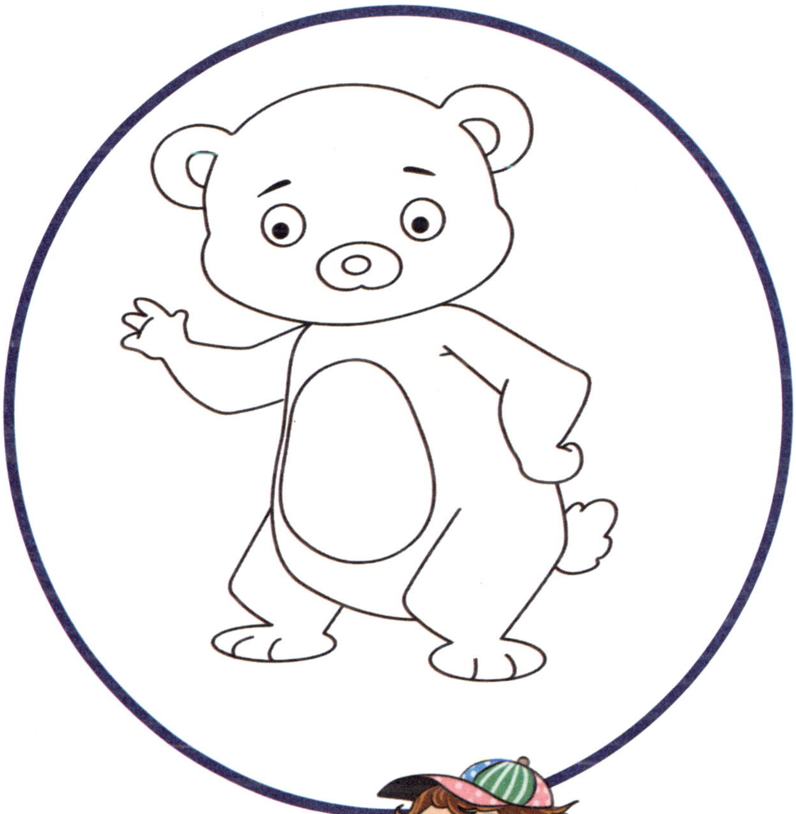

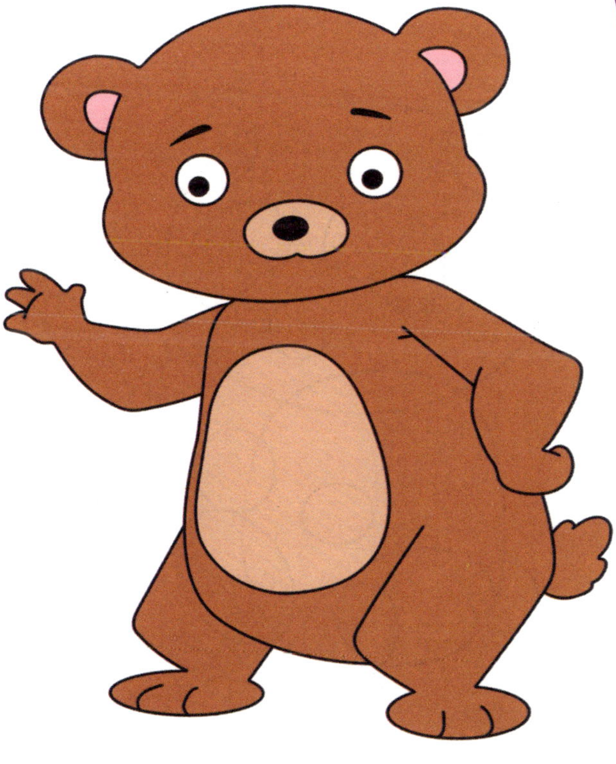

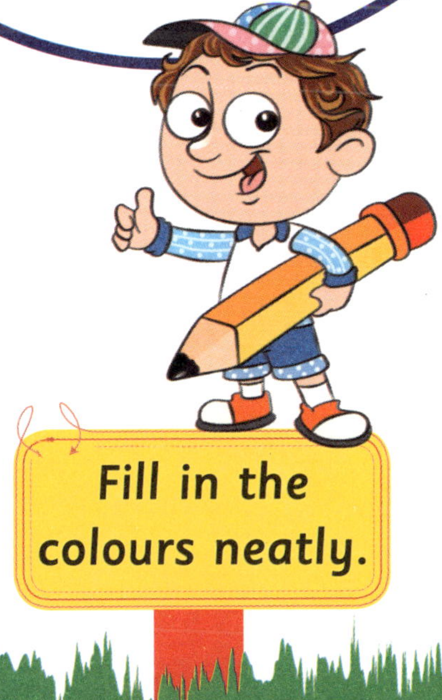

Panda

STEP 1 2 3 4

A panda is popular for the big, black patch around its eyes. It is a very good climber.

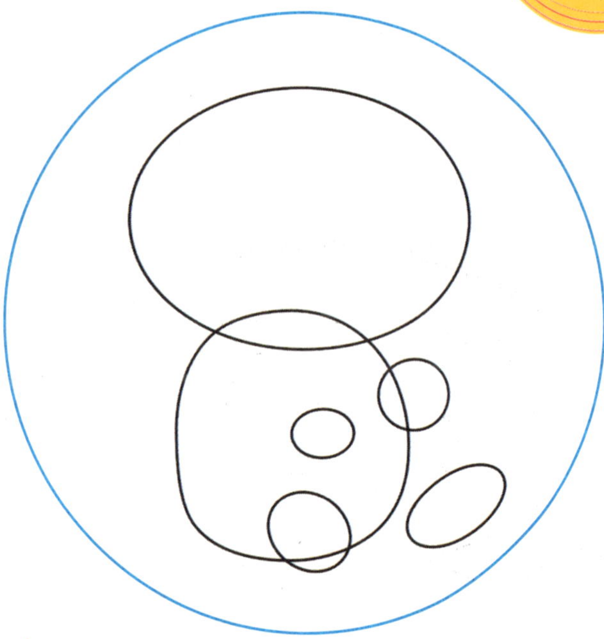

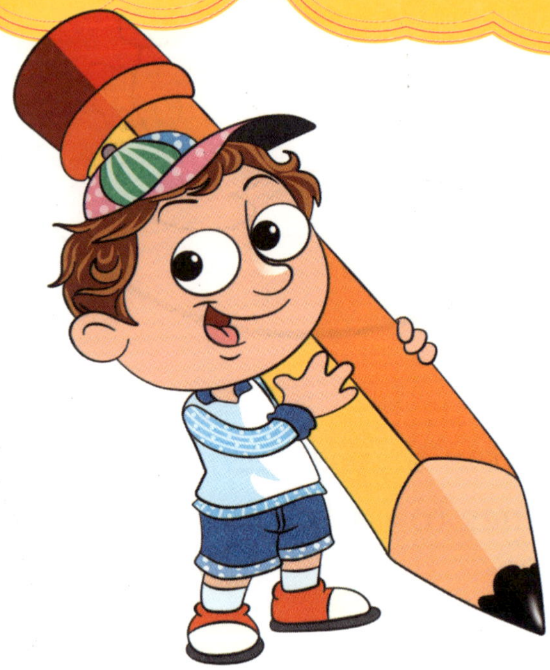

1 Draw two big circles for the head and body. Draw smaller circles for its paws.

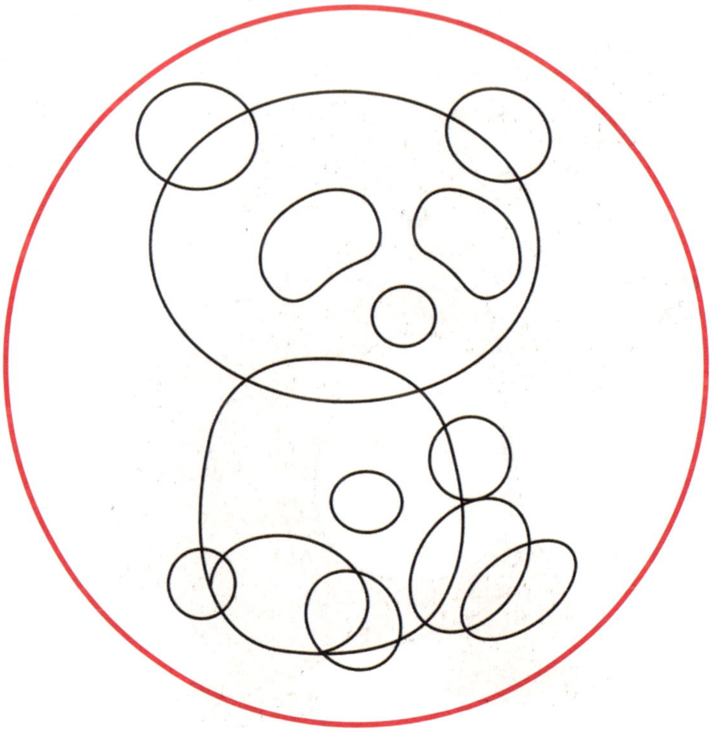

2 Add in more shapes for the eyes, face, ears, legs and tail.

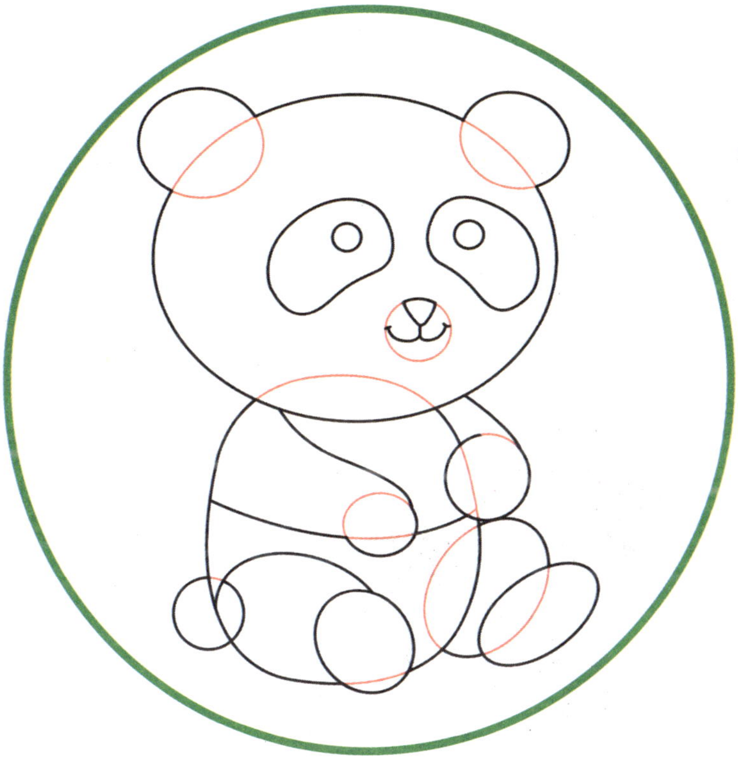

3 Draw its eyes, mouth, nose, arms, body and legs. Erase the unwanted lines (marked in red).

4 Draw the insides of its eyes and ears.

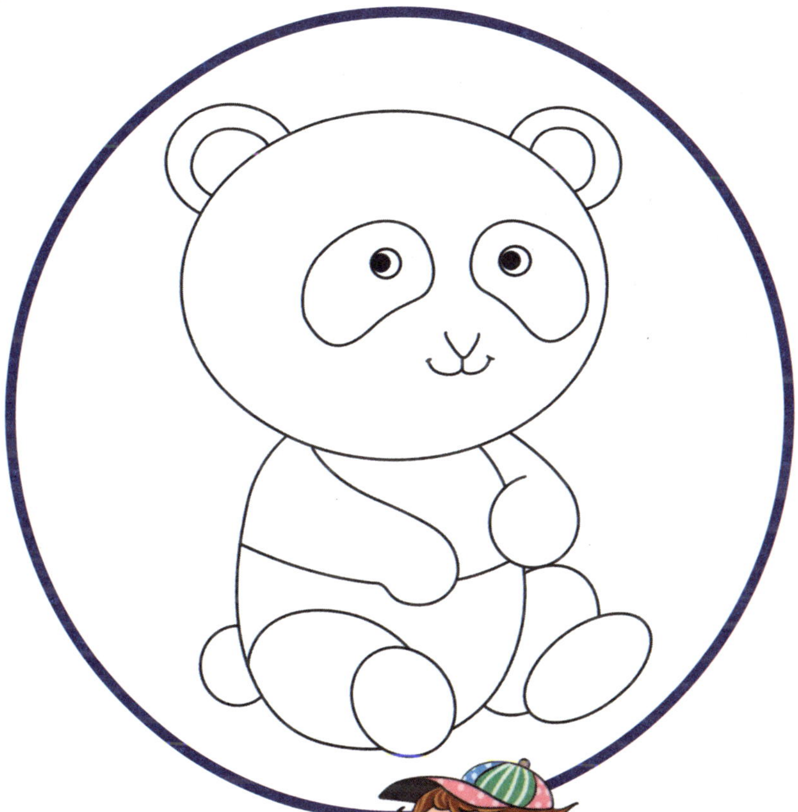

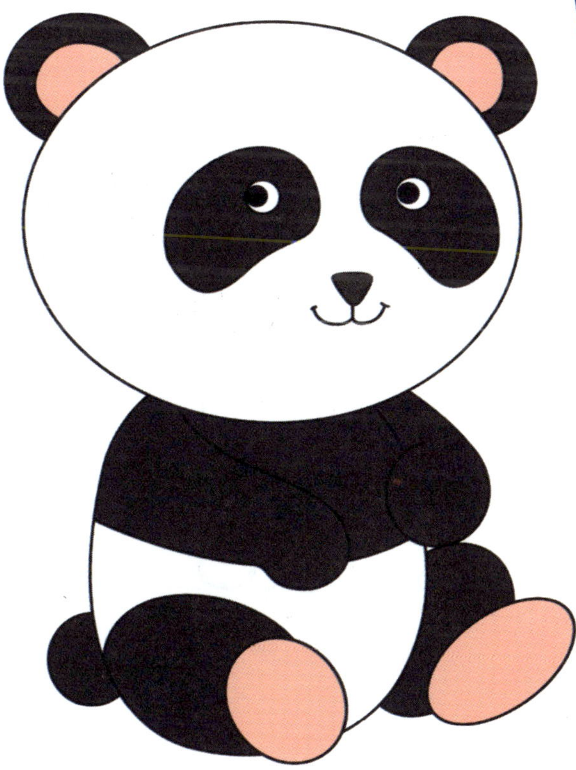

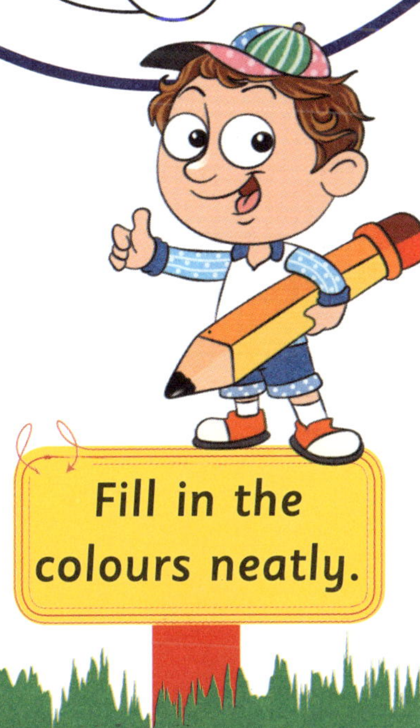

Sheep

STEP 1 2 3 4

It is a farm animal. It is reared for its wool. A baby sheep is called a lamb.

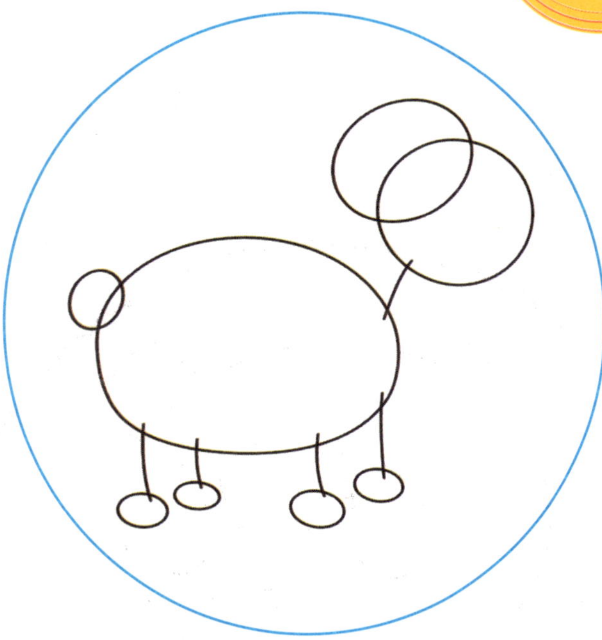

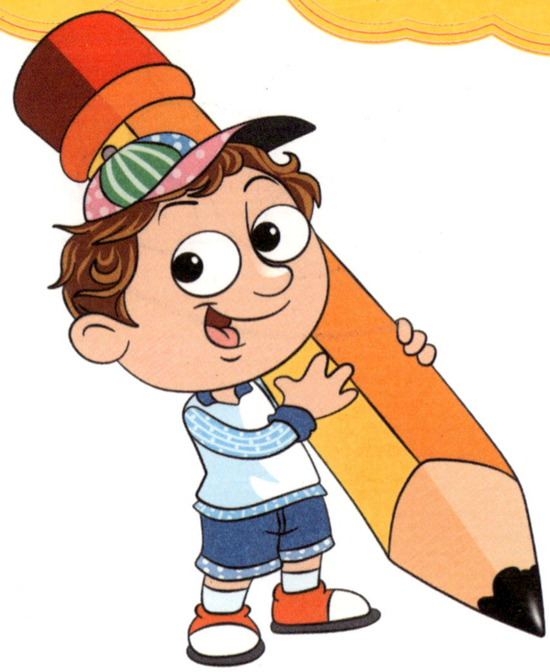

1 Draw two circles for the hair and the face. Draw an oval for the body. Draw five small circles for the feet and tail. Draw lines for the neck and legs.

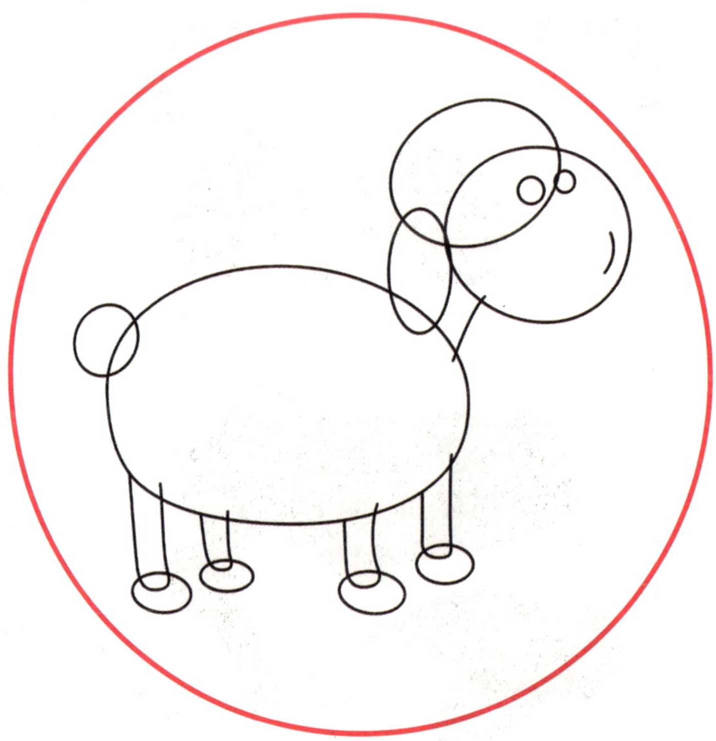

2 Draw in the legs, ear and eyes.

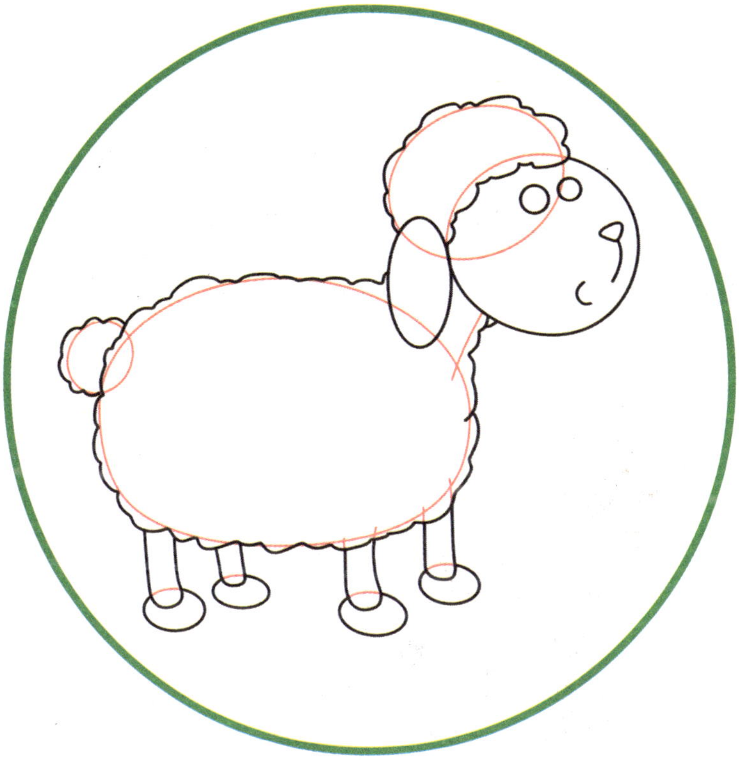

3 Draw its mouth, nose, hair, tail, neck and body. Erase the unwanted lines (marked in red).

4 Fill in the eyes. Draw in the eyebrows and lines for the feet and body.

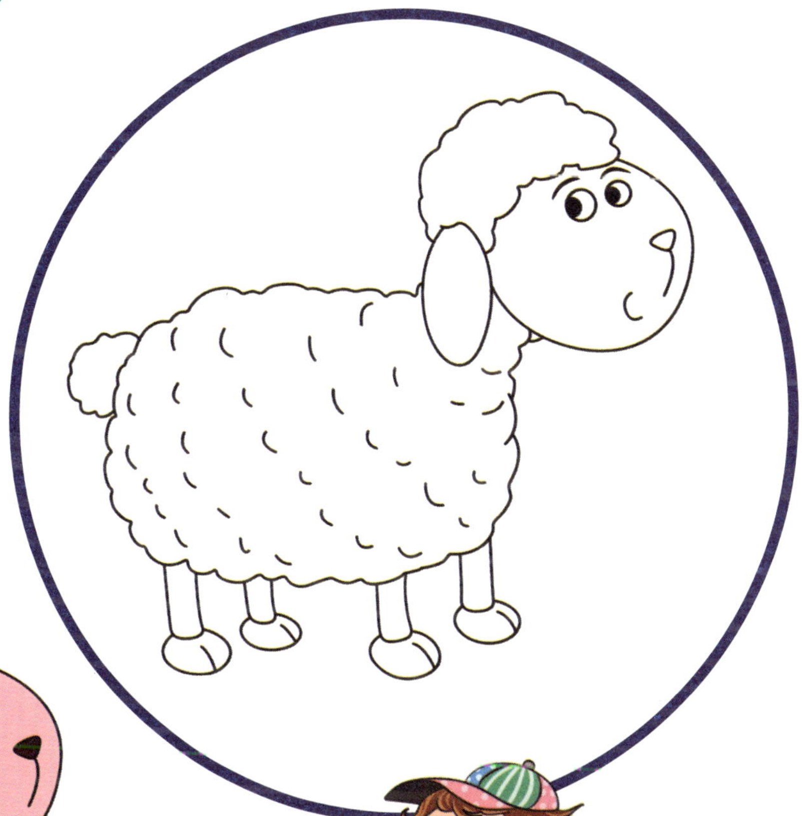

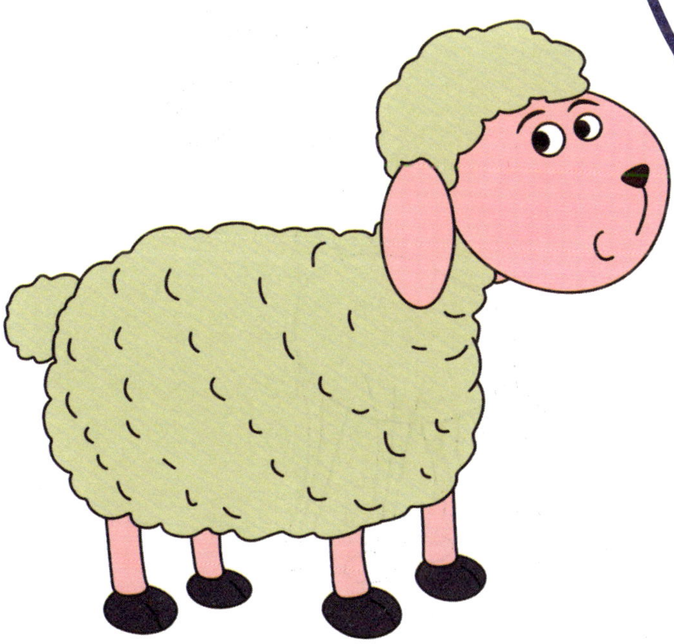

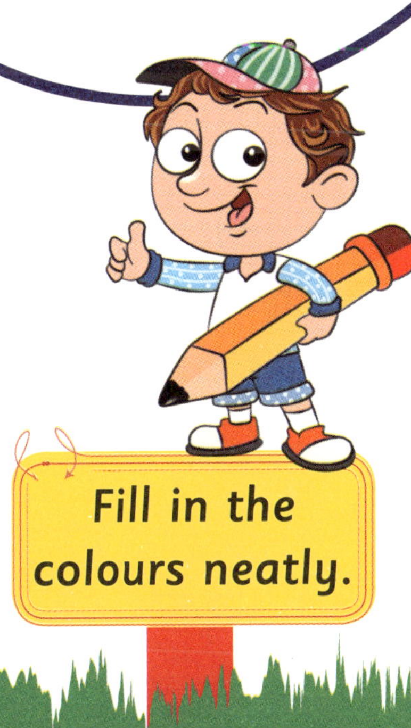

Giraffe

STEP 1 2 3 4

A giraffe is the tallest living animal in the world as it has a really long neck. It can sleep while standing!

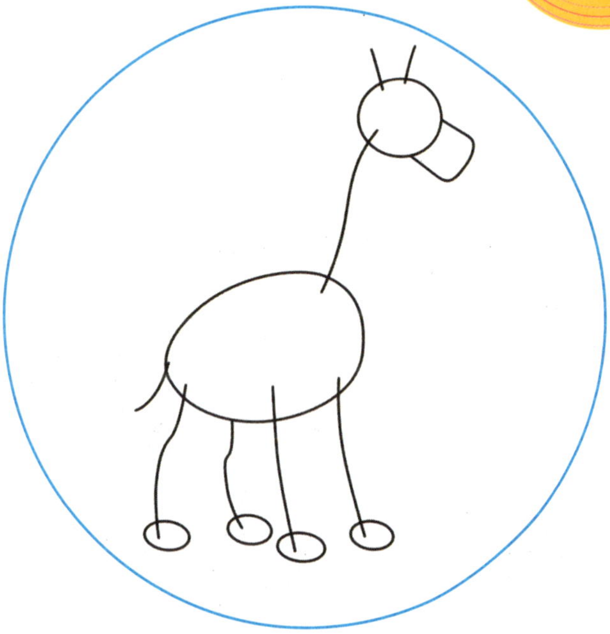

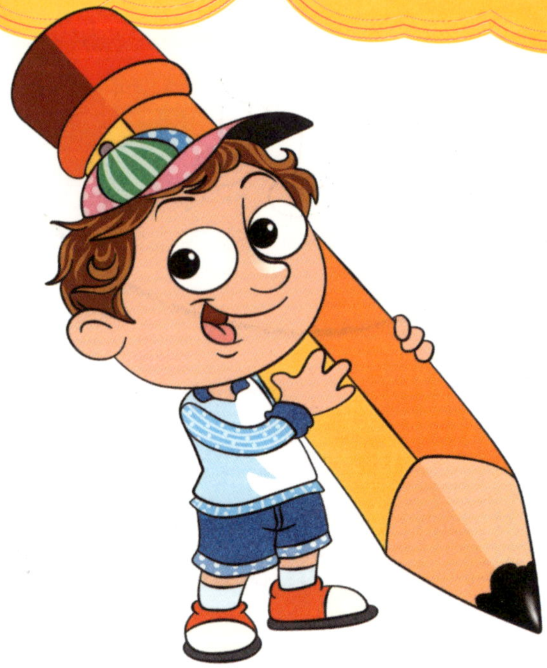

1. Draw a circle for the head and curved square for the mouth. Draw one big circle for its body and four small circles for the feet. Draw lines for the horns, neck, tail and legs.

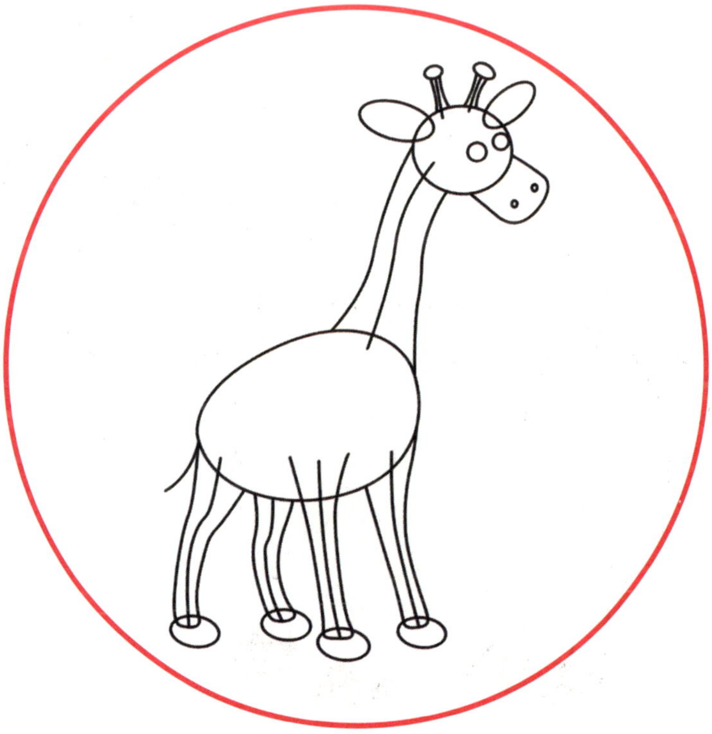

2. Add lines for the horns, ears, neck, nose, eyes, face, body, legs and feet.

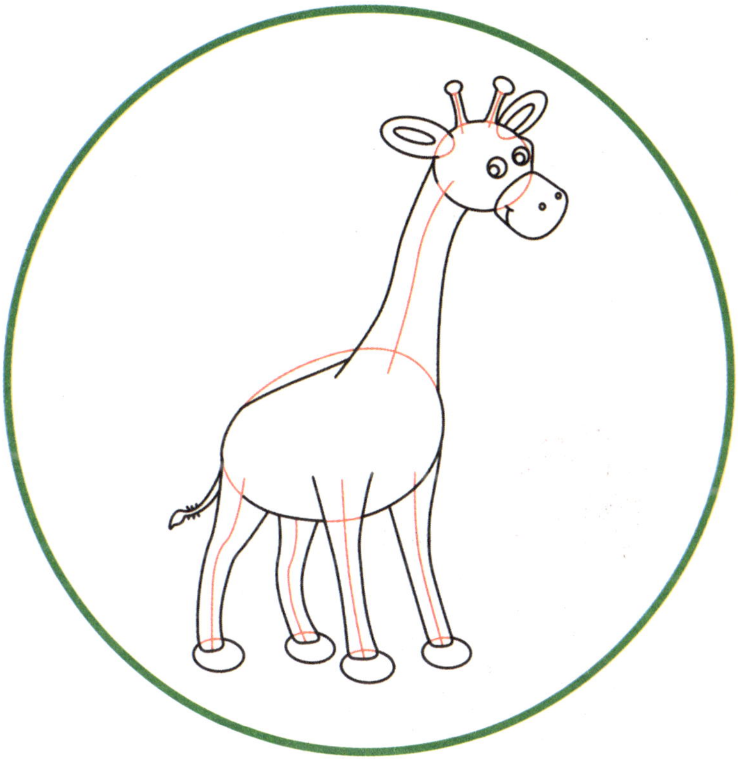

3 Draw the insides of the eyes and ears. Draw its tail and mouth. Erase the unwanted lines (marked in red).

4 Draw in the eyebrows, spots on its neck and body and lines for its feet.

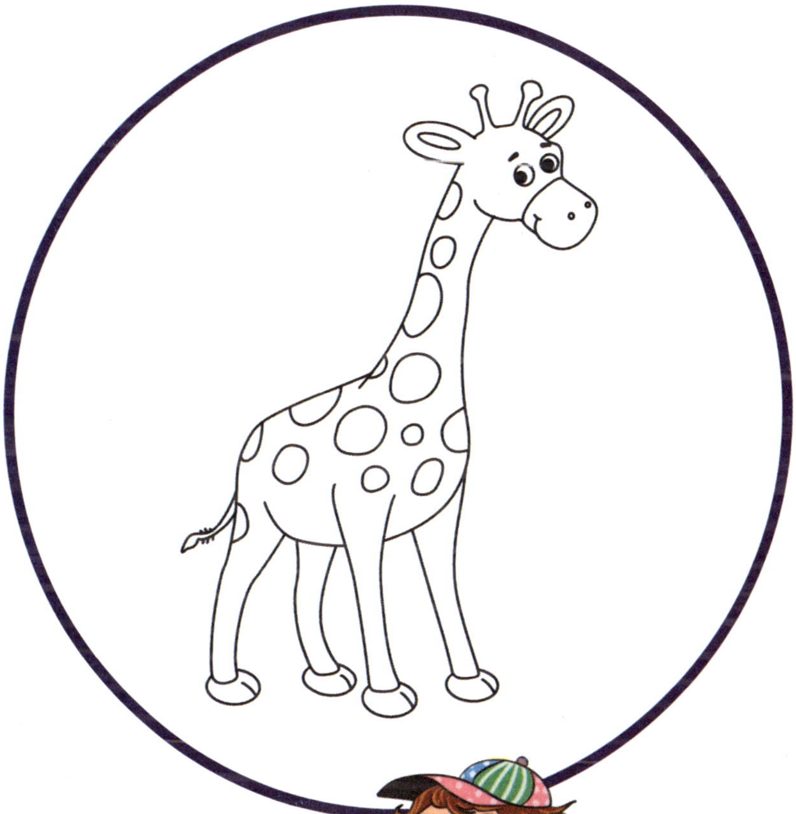

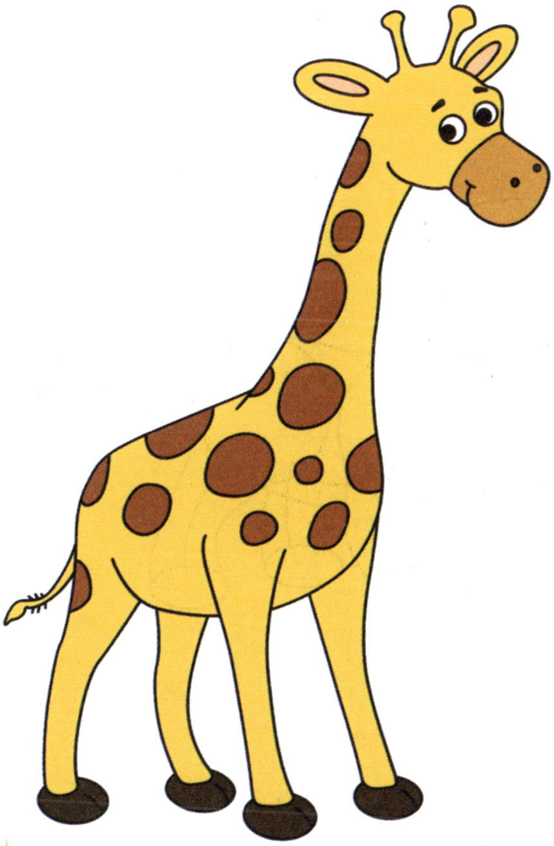

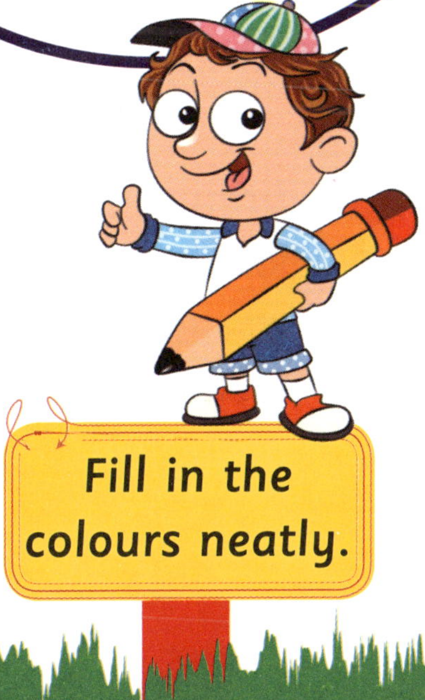

Tiger

STEP 1 2 3 4

It is the largest animal among cats. It only eats flesh. A baby tiger is a cub.

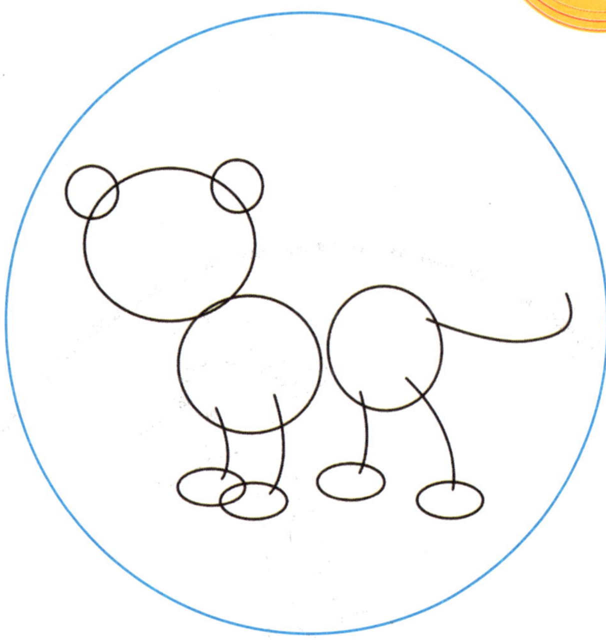

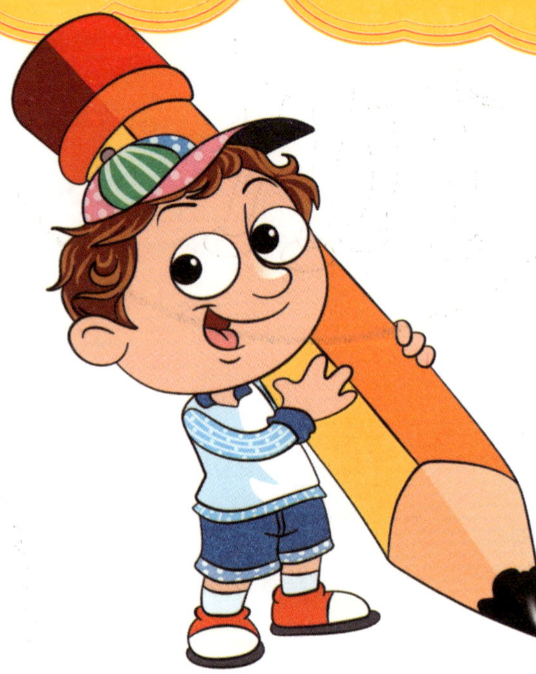

1. Draw a circle for the face. Draw two small circles for the ears and two circles one after the other for the body. Draw lines for the legs and tail and four small circles for the feet.

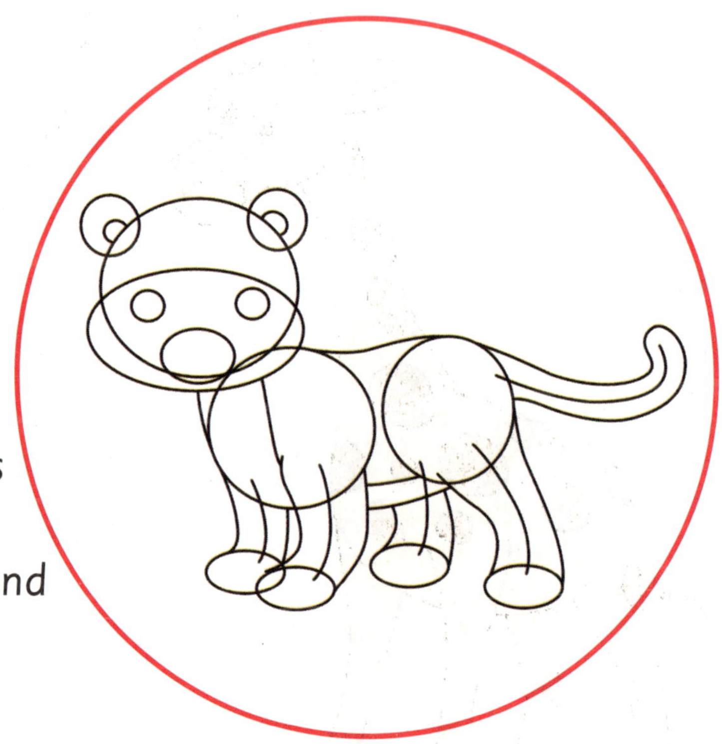

2. Draw in smaller circles for the ears, eyes and an oval for the nose and mouth. Draw the tail, body, feet and legs.

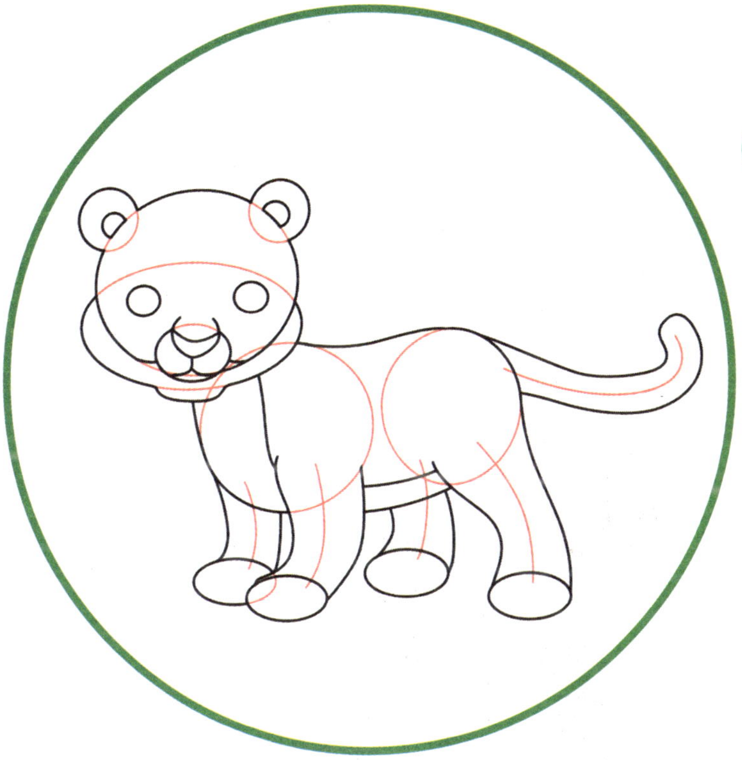

3 Draw the mouth, nose and face.
Erase the unwanted lines (marked in red).

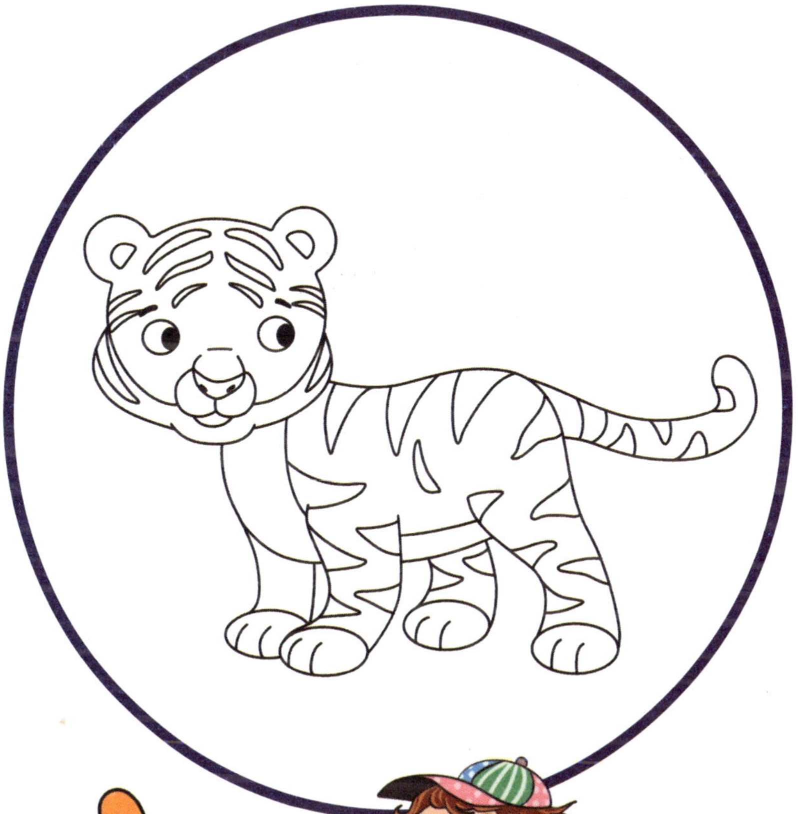

4 Draw in stripes, eyebrows and fill in the eyes. Put in dots for the nose and lines for its feet.

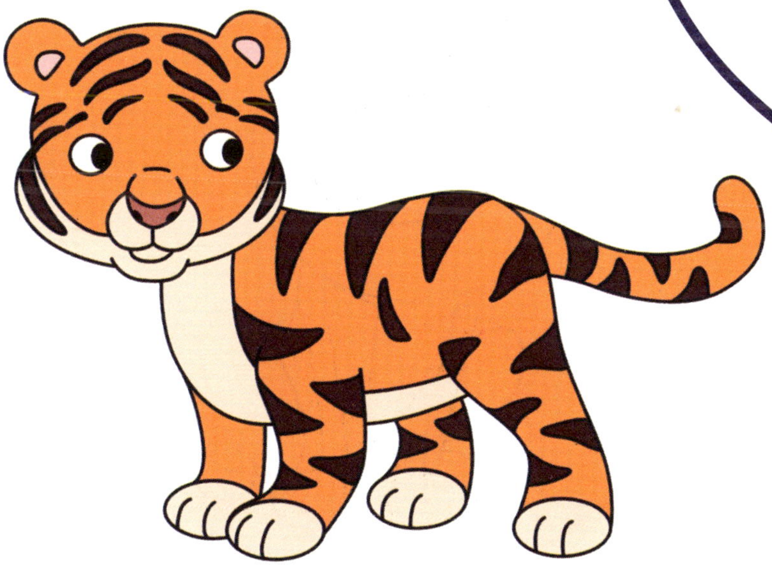

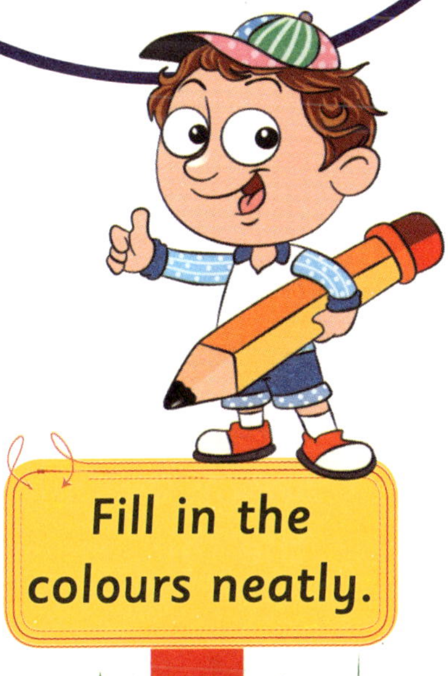

Lion

STEP 1 2 3 4

A lion lives in groups of 10 to 15 lions and these are called 'prides'. A baby lion is a cub, whelp or lionet.

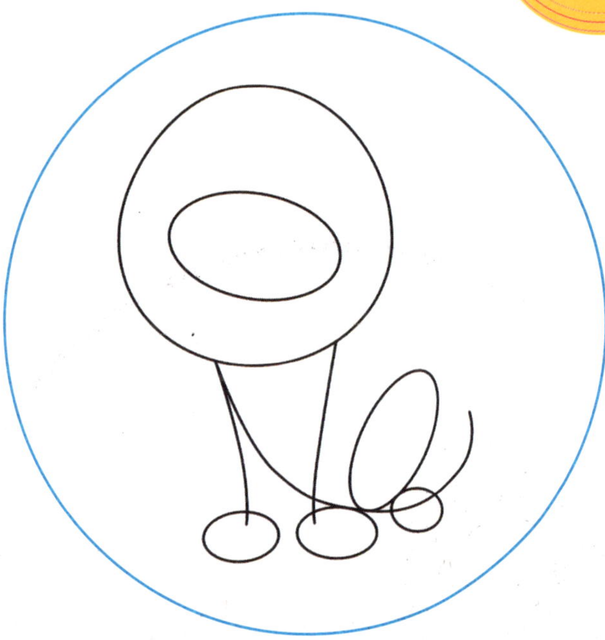

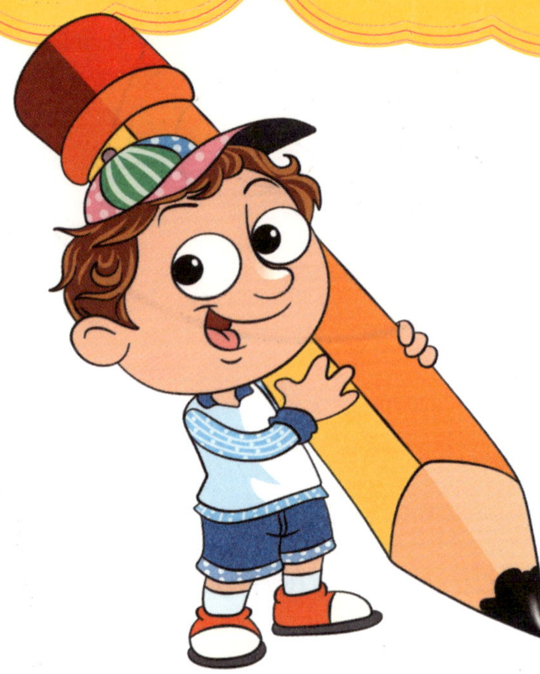

1 Draw a circle and an oval inside it for the head. Draw in small circles for its paws and an oval for its leg. Draw lines for its legs, body and tail.

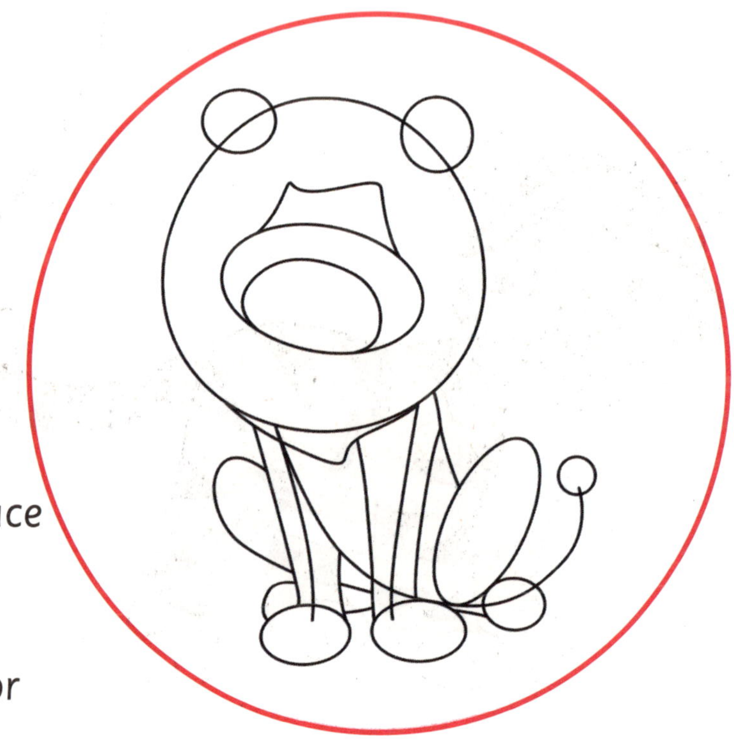

2 Draw in the ears and more shapes for its face and hair. Draw the legs, paws and body. Draw a small circle for the tail.

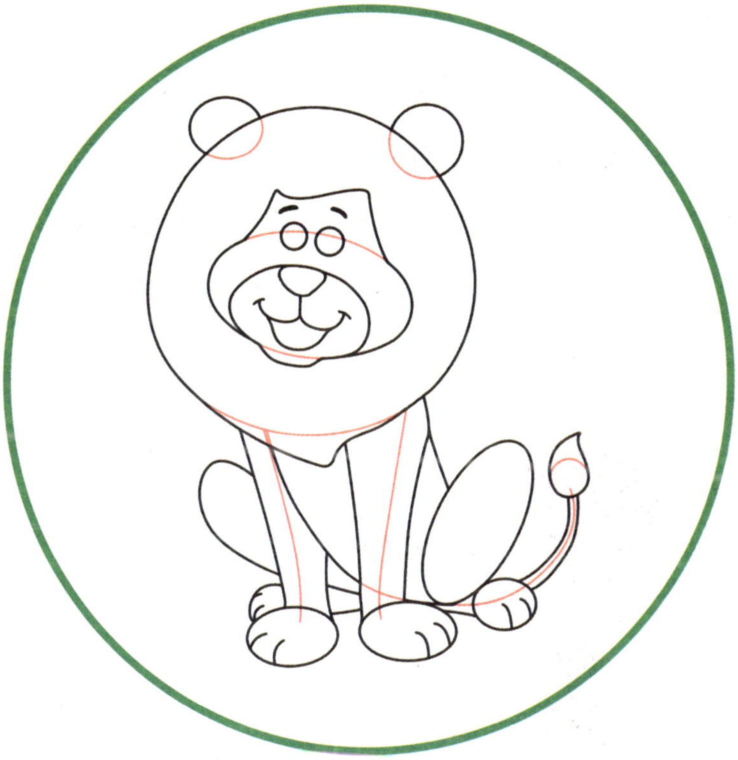

3 Draw in its eyes, eyebrows, nose, face details and mouth. Draw the tail and lines of the paws. Erase the unwanted lines (marked in red).

4 Add lines to the ears. Draw the tongue and fill in the eyes.

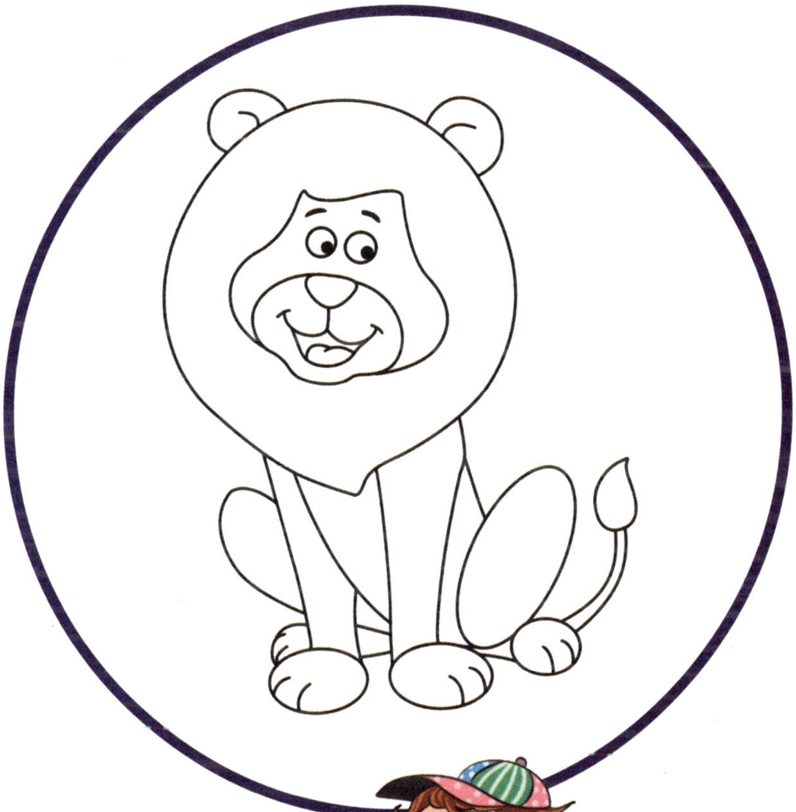

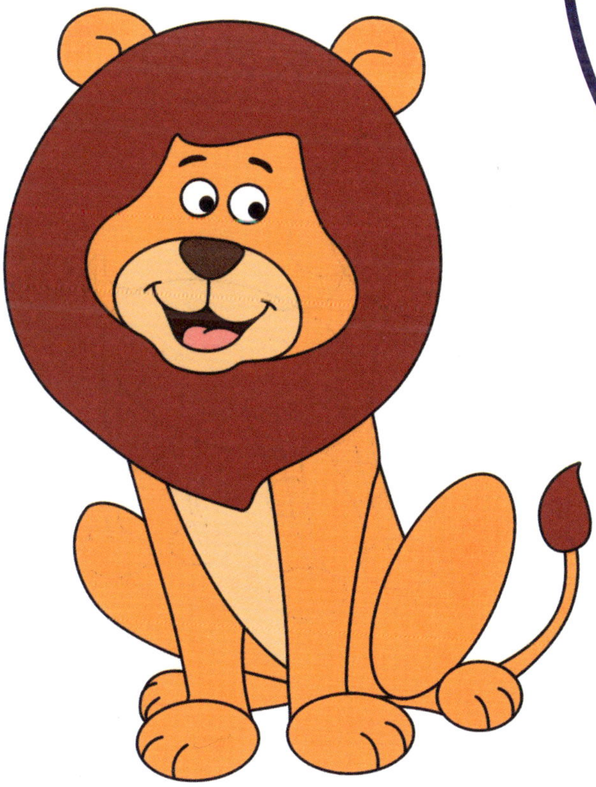

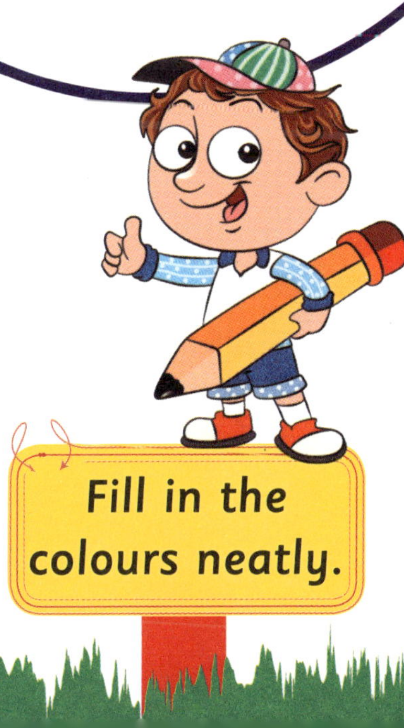

Goat

STEP 1 2 3 4

A male goat is called a buck or billy, female goat is called a nanny or doe and the baby goat is called a kid.

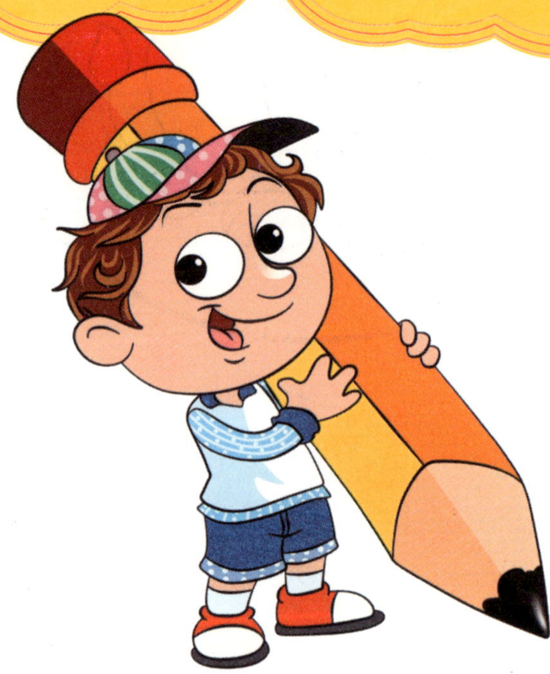

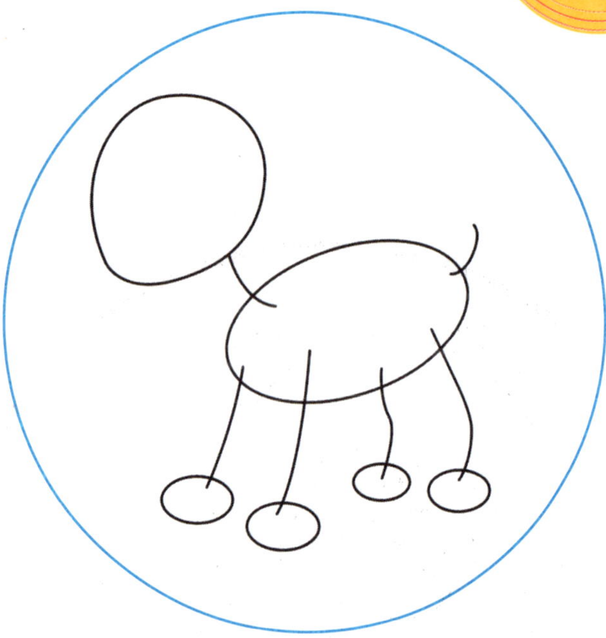

1. Draw a pear shape for the head and an oval for the body. Draw four small circles for the feet. Draw lines for the neck, tail and legs.

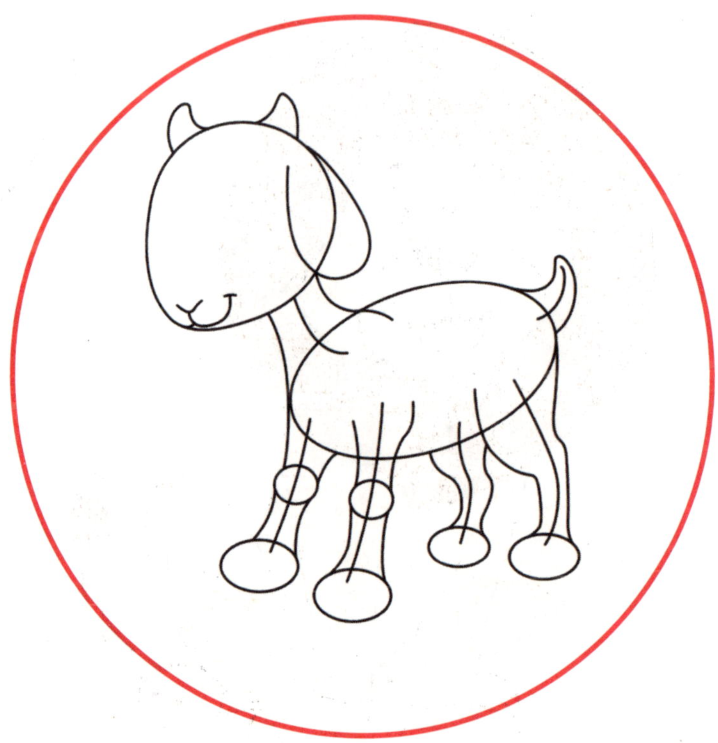

2. Draw in the horns, ears, nose, mouth, neck, body, tail, legs and feet.

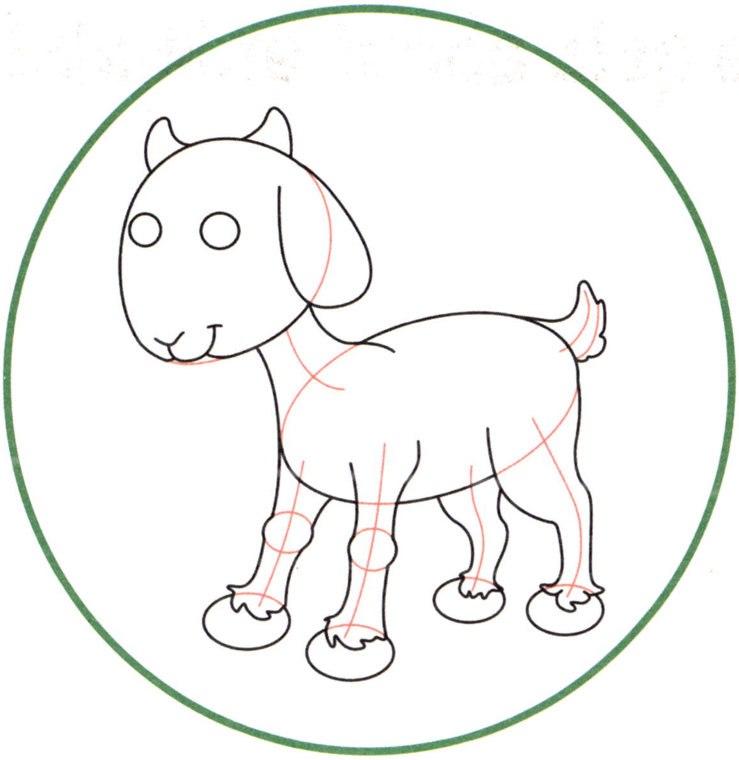

3 Draw in its eyes and shape for its tail and feet. Erase the unwanted lines (marked in red).

4 Draw in the eyebrows and lines for the feet. Fill in the eyes.

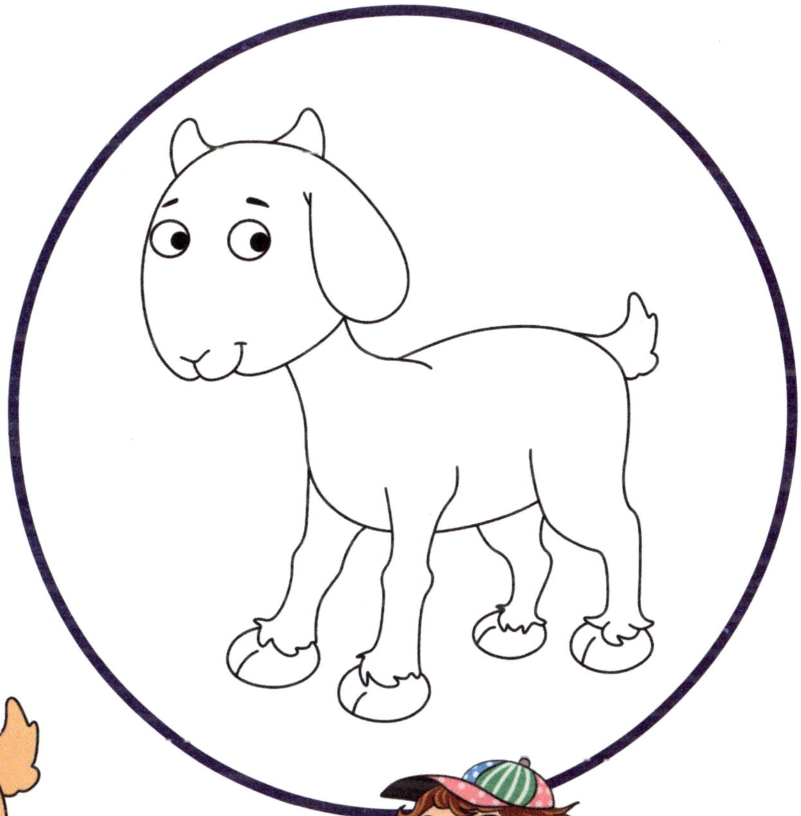

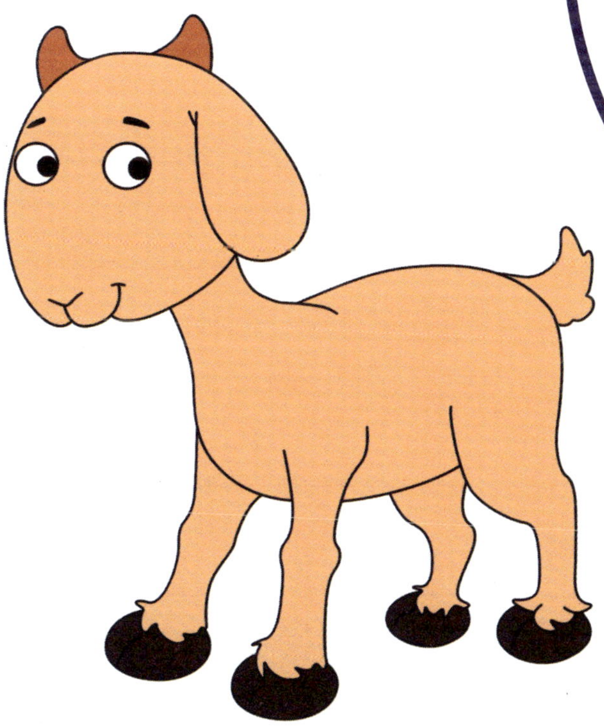

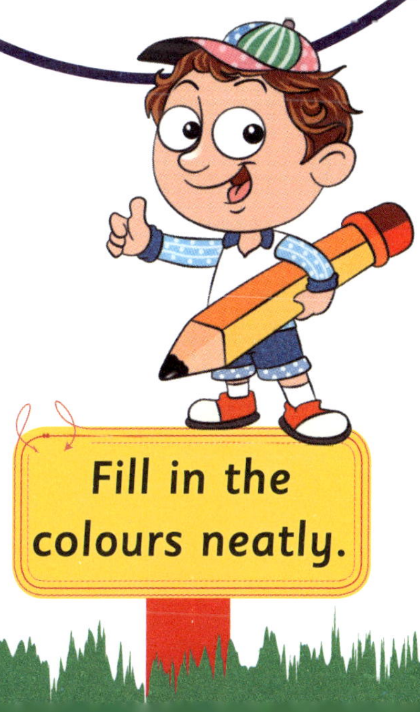

Let's have fun with a quiz about animals!

STEP 1 2 3 4

1. Which animal has a long trunk?
2. Who is man's best friend?
3. Who has fins?
4. Who loves to drink milk?
5. Which animal loves to eat bananas?
6. Who loves to eat carrots?
7. Who has big eyes and a bushy tail?
8. Who loves to eat cheese?
9. Who has big black patches around its eyes?
10. Who sleeps for six months in the winter?
11. Who lives in prides?
12. Which is a farm animal?
13. Which is the tallest animal?
14. Who eats flesh?
15. Whose baby animal is called kid?